FRIGHT BASH

THE FRIGHT SERIES

LANDRY HILL

FRIGHT BASH

Lexie

We've been best friends since we were kids. Practically raised together like brother and sister. But one night, a line is crossed. Now, things between us have changed.

Our friendship is walking a tight rope. And that rope frays when Jaxon does the unforgivable. Now I'm not sure we'll ever get back what we lost.

Or... if my heart will ever recover.

CHAPTER 1

Lexie

"Thanks for dinner, Mom. We're going to head up to my room and watch a movie while y'all duke it out over charades."

"Wait. What?" Mrs. Miller comes walking out of the kitchen, holding a bottle of wine in her hands. "We need you on our team, Lex. It's girls against guys tonight."

I glance over at Jax, biting back my laugh. If our moms are drinking wine, then things are going to get sloppy-silly real fast. And as much fun as it is to watch the two lightweights struggle to act out their cards and burst into rolling fits of giggles, I'm tired tonight. We had an eight-hour cheerleading practice today to get ready for the homecoming game, and I'm pooped. My body is sore and my brain is mush. But the homecoming half-time show is going to be *fire*.

"You two go on up and watch your movie," Dad chimes in. "Us men need a fighting chance."

"Speak for yourself, Dave," Mr. Miller teases, taking the bottle from his wife's hands and twisting the corkscrew into the top. "We'd easily be able to take them down with Jaxon on our team. My boy's a genius."

"Okay, we're out." Jax smirks, shaking his head. "You kids have fun, and no fighting. Remember it's only a game."

His comment has me giggling as I turn to head upstairs. That's exactly what our parents used to always tell us when we were kids. Though, their warning never stuck. We'd still get into the biggest fights, just like brother and sister. But it was inevitable based on how much time we were forced to spend together.

We didn't just have to see each other during family dinner night every Sunday; our moms had us enrolled in the same preschool class, music class, summer camps, and library reading group. They even had us in the same dance class—which I absolutely hated. I wanted to be the star of the show, but Jaxon would come out on stage dressed in a mini tuxedo, wiggling his hips with a big goofy grin on his face, and the audience would go crazy over him. They wouldn't even see my performance, just the cute boy fumbling around in the middle of the stage.

But once Jaxon became interested in football, everything changed. All of his activities started to revolve around the sport. And once we were no longer forced at the hip every waking hour of the day, we missed each other. Now, we're attached at the hip because we want to be.

"Here. You pick." I grab the remote from my desk and toss it on the bed for him.

"Nah, you pick, Lexie Lou. You're the one who had the brutal day."

He turns on the TV, scrolling to my movie account, while I walk into my closet to change. I slip off my jeans and slink on some flannel pajama pants, then toss my shirt into my laundry basket on my way out, walking over to my dresser and grabbing a tank top from my drawer.

"Hey," I turn towards him, pulling my shirt right side out,

"what about the new *Kissing Booth* movie? I haven't seen the third one yet. Have you?"

He doesn't answer. I'm guessing that means he's not a fan of my suggestion. "I told you you could pick, Jax."

I look up from my shirt, but as soon as I see his face, I no longer think my movie choice is the reason for his silence. Something else has caught his undivided attention. My tits. He's staring directly at my chest, tongue practically hanging out of his mouth—shocking me with his reaction.

It's not like Jax hasn't seen me in my bra before. I change in front of him all the time. He's also seen me in a bikini ever since we were toddlers. But never once has he ever shown any interest in my boobs—or my body. He's always looked at me as just a friend, like a kid sister. Yet, right now, the look in his eyes is anything but platonic.

My brow cocks up, wondering what on earth is going through my best friend's head. "What? Did you just realize I have boobs, Jax?"

His eyes snap up to mine and he shakes his head like he's shaking himself out of a trance, looking sheepishly adorable with his now blushing cheeks. "Sorry. Didn't mean to stare. But you know you have killer tits, right?"

I jut my chest out further, preening at his compliment. I used to think I was small in the boob department, especially in comparison to Piper and her ridonckulously huge knockers, but I've grown to appreciate my little Bs. They make clothes shopping easy, and they don't get in the way when I'm jumping around during cheer. Plus, all the guys I've dated seemed to like them.

But I'll admit, I've never been this flattered before. Which has me mentally scratching my head.

"They are good, aren't they," I agree, dismissing the awkward thought. "But you need to put that tongue back inside your mouth, bucko. Best friends are not allowed to look, or drool."

I give him a wink before pulling my tank top down over my head. When I pop back up through the neck hole, he's still staring at me, only the look on his face is even more intense.

A shiver ripples down my spine and decides to settle right between my legs. *What the heck?* I'm not supposed to be turned on by him. It's Jaxon Miller. My best friend. A boy I've known my entire life.

Sure, he's drop-dead gorgeous. A ripped specimen of female fantasy perfection. Super tall. Broad shouldered. Dark brown hair. The dreamiest blue eyes you've ever seen. And a killer smile that has all the girls on my squad melting into a puddle every time he casts one in their direction. BUT...he's like my brother. He's not someone who should be causing my lady bits to get all tingly.

"If you don't want me looking, Lex, then you shouldn't change in front of me." His brow goes up in challenge, his voice dropping an octave. It feels like he's flirting with me. What in the world?

Again, since when has Jaxon even noticed I'm a female? Our moms used to put us in the bath together as kids, and he'd never even point out our differences. We used to jump in the pool naked and not once would he peek a curious glance in my direction. He's never shown any interest and certainly has never looked at me the way he is right now. Nor has my body ever had this kind of reaction to him before.

But maybe it's because we've both been on the single train for a while. Maybe our raging teenage hormones have momentarily taken over our brains and there's a glitch in the system. At least, that's the excuse I'm going with as I reach my hand up under the back of my shirt and unhook my bra, pulling the straps through my arm holes, then letting it drop to the ground. My eyes never leaving his once. His, on the other hand, land right on my peaked nipples and stare openly; making them tighter under the heat of his attention.

4

"I'm fully dressed, and yet you're still staring, Jax." I walk toward the bed, giving him a better view the closer I get. The thin ribbed white cotton reveals the size and shade of my pink nipples. God, I've worn this shirt around him dozens of times and never once gave any thought to him seeing me in it. Never once thought about the fact that it's practically see-through. And he's never once homed in so intensely.

He finally looks up when I step in front of him, the hunger in his eyes sending goose bumps up my arms.

"Can't help it." He unabashedly looks back down at my two peaked mounds. "They're pointing right at me. I think they like my attention." His tongue runs across his lower lip, and another burst of heat spreads to the parts of my body that are completely off-limits to our friendship. "Damn, Lex."

His groan sends a hot wave of lust rolling through me. My panties are now getting damp and my nipples are tingling. This is definitely wrong and has already gone way too far. I need to stop flirting with my *best friend* and break the tension in this inappropriately charged moment before we cross a line.

I quickly reach out, grabbing the pillow off my bed and whack him with it. Jaxon nearly falls back, not expecting my surprise attack, and I burst into giggles. But I let down my guard too soon because he shoots back up with my other pillow in hand and nearly takes me down with one blow. Jax is definitely stronger than me, but I'm faster. I whack him again and then grab his pillow and try to tug it from him, but my sore shoulders quickly remind me of the extra-long workout I had today, and a groan slips out.

"Shit. You okay, Lex?"

"Yeah." I nod, dropping my hold from the plush weapon. "Just super sore from today." I hold up my hands in surrender. "Truce?"

He lays his pillow down on the bed then pats it. "Come. Lie down and I'll massage your shoulders."

I crawl onto the bed and sprawl out for him while he picks up the remote and scrolls through to find the movie. I'm just thankful the awkwardness of a moment ago is gone. I'm still not sure what that was all about, but based on my crazy reaction, I definitely think it's time to find myself a boyfriend. Only problem is: there's no one at our school I'm interested in. And the few I did have a thing for, ended up being complete duds.

Not only were they immature, but they sucked in bed. And the only one who was decent in that department—although, still mediocre—ended up being a complete douche nugget. Jeff laughed his ass off when I fell from the top of the pyramid during a routine. And while he was rolling in hysterics, pointing at me from the stands, Jax came running off the field mid-game, lifting me off the ground and making sure I was okay.

Needless to say, I broke up with Jeff that night. Although, I should've broken it off sooner. Nine times out of ten when he'd take me out on a date, we'd end up at the basketball court and he'd join in on a pick-up game, leaving me bored on the sidelines for hours. At least if Jaxon ever takes me to the court to shoot around, he'll play HORSE with me and make it fun.

Jax climbs up onto the back of my thighs, straddling me as the movie starts to play. But as soon as his strong fingers dive into my aching muscles, my head flops to the side and I get lost in the feeling, the movie completely forgotten as he rubs and kneads all the knots away, making my body turn to puddy as he hits every single tight pressure point.

"You know," I moan as he finds another lump of tension along my shoulder blade and massages the pain away. "If football doesn't work out for you, you could totally be a massage therapist."

"I'll keep that in mind." He chuckles. "By the way, how'd the girls like the new routine?"

I smile at the thought of the squad's excitement. "They loved it. And they're seriously excited about the new uniforms I ordered, too."

"Figured they would be." He shifts to my other shoulder, giving it the same amazing treatment. "You know if event planning doesn't work out for you, you could totally become a dance choreographer."

Once upon a time, that's exactly what I dreamt of doing. I envisioned owning my own dance studio and being able to choreograph recitals. I wanted to put on the most spectacular holiday show this city has ever seen and give girls like me a chance to show off their talents. I dreamt of Juilliard and all the best schools knocking on my door, scouting for their next stars. And having a waitlist of dancers wanting to take classes from me. But unfortunately…that dream got flushed down the toilet after my feud with Sienna.

That's the year I quit dance and took up cheerleading instead. I was done with the drama. Now, I'm the captain of the cheer team and get to cheer *and* dance. Plus, I get to spend more time with Jax. But I'd be lying if I said there wasn't a part of me that doesn't miss my old dance studio and being up on that stage. Letting my body flow to the beat. Telling a story with movement and feeling the thrill when the last note hits and the audience stands, giving a roaring applause.

"Speaking of party planning," I say, returning my focus on Jaxon's incredible hands and trying to block out those uncomfortable feelings, which are sneaking back in. His fingers are now working their way down the center of my back, thumbs running pressure along my spine. "We still need to go shopping for the Fright Bash. And I need to pick out my costume for it."

I'm getting so excited for the party. Jaxon's decided to go big for our senior year and has enlisted the entire JV football team to haunt his "graveyard." Which means we need to buy a lot more decorations.

"We can go shopping this week." His magical hands press

into another knot, loosening me further. "By the way, Mr. Baxter told me I could borrow anything he's retired from the Fright House. So I'll take a look when I'm on shift this week."

"Oh, that's so awesome." Which reminds me. "I'm going to try to round up the girls to come to the Fright House this Friday. Are you working that night?"

"Yeah, we're all on shift this weekend since it's a bi-week."

Guess I should've figured as much. Practically the entire football team works at the Fright House, so when they don't have a game, they're all at "work" scaring the crap out of people. I still can't believe I've never been, but this time of year is always hectic with cheer competitions. But since this may be my last chance to go, I'm not missing out.

"You feeling better, Lexie Lou?"

"Yes," I groan. "Much."

"Any place else you need me to massage?" His fingers trail down my sides, inching a little too close to my breasts as they slide back up.

"Careful, mister," I scold. "You're getting a little too close to the goods."

His hands follow the same path again, ignoring my warning. "You know you like it, Lex. Don't even try to pretend."

It's true. I do like it. Every single one of his touches feels amazing. And I shouldn't have said that. He's massaged me like this dozens of times and I've never had a problem with it in the past. I'm the one making this weird when it doesn't have to be. I just need to close my mouth and relax. Although, that's a little hard to do when my body is starting to tingle again.

"You know," he says, shifting himself lower down my legs. "I've heard that our butts hold the most stress of our bodies." His fingers press into my cheeks and I let out a moan as a knot of soreness eases away. Now, this he's never done before. But there's no way I'm going to tell him to stop; it feels too incredible.

"I think you're right," I gasp as he kneads into me with more pressure. "Oh my God, that feels so good, Jax. I think I did a thousand squats today." A thousand squats and a thousand hip thrusts.

"Yeah, it definitely feels tight."

His voice sounds lower, raspier. He must be putting all his strength into this massage.

He shifts again, switching to the other side, pressing into my other sore cheek, and I swear I feel his dick pressing into my leg. *Long. Big. And so...HARD.* He's turned on by this. By touching me. Or maybe our little moment is still causing a lingering effect.

My body strums back to life. The heat coursing through my veins. But if I tell him to stop, it'll only make things awkward between us again. He'll ask me why, and then what? It's not like I'm going to tell him it's because his hard-on is totally turning *me* on. No. I think it's best to keep quiet and try focusing on the tension he's releasing from my muscles and not the tension he's causing between my legs.

But as his hands move lower, gripping closer to my center, it becomes harder to focus on anything other than the ache forming in the pit of my stomach. And when he starts digging in with his thumbs, pushing and pulling my skin in such a way that the pleasure starts to increase, slowly building my orgasm, I lose the grip on my control and a moan purrs from my throat before I can bury my head into the pillow and muffle it.

"Feel good, Lex?"

I bob my head, face planted in my pillowcase, not wanting to speak and give myself away.

He moves lower, his efforts doubling. The pressure of his thumbs... The rubbing of my folds... All of it is making me dizzy with lust. I'm not sure if he knows what he's doing to me. Not sure if he can sense my body's reaction. But if he doesn't stop, I'm going to be coming soon.

9

"Yes, it feels good," I groan, trying to get ahold of myself. "But it hurts higher up on the sides. More towards my hips."

I'm desperately trying to avert what's happening, but Jaxon's fingers seem to be ignoring my request. His thumbs keep running along the underside of my butt cheeks, swiping awfully close to my center and sending another set of tingles ricocheting off my nerves. The pleasure's building fast. My hips are fighting the urge not to thrust against the bed, wanting to get the pressure against my clit.

"I think this is the part that needs my attention most," he rasps, his breathing even heavier. "It hurts, doesn't it?"

Oh God. It does. I'm struggling to keep up the pretense, trying not to cross a line and thrust my hips back to get him to touch where it hurts the most, biting my tongue so I don't beg him to massage my clit. Again, I nod my head, fighting not to let another moan slip free. But when his thumbs accidentally slip between my legs, I fail to hide my body's reaction.

A moan comes clawing from the pit of my aching gut, my fingers gripping into my comforter as the pleasure takes over. I expect him to pull his hands away, apologizing for his slipup, but he doesn't. His hands stay wedged between my legs, thumbs now rubbing over my folds. Holy shit. This can't be happening. But it is. And God, does it feel good.

"Fuck, Lex. You're so wet, baby."

I'm not sure what's happening between us, why he's driving the tension forward. All I know is I'm too weak to put a stop to it. My body has given up the fight and my hips are now seeking more pressure. Thrusting toward the pleasure. Grinding down and squirming against my sheets, desperate for relief.

He shifts behind me, the weight of his heavy chest coming over my back. His hot breath grazing my ear. "Raise your hips," his gruff voice commands.

I follow his order, ignoring that tiny voice in my head telling me I should put an end to this craziness. That I need to draw the line before we go too far and ruin our friendship. But that rational thought gets blurred out when his hand slips inside the front of my pants and his thick fingers slide straight to my clit. He gives me just the right amount of pressure, pressing down and rubbing back and forth, then pinching the tight bud between two fingers and fidgeting me into a frenzy. It's like he's attuned to my body and knows exactly how to make me feel incredible.

"This little clit feels like she's been neglected, Lex." His hot rasp sends a rush of tingles through me. He's breathing just as hard as I am. God, he has no idea. None of the guys I've been with were this skilled. Even my own fingers aren't this perfect.

I reach my arm back, bracing the base of his head, clutching onto his hair. "You shouldn't be touching me like this, Jax." My breathless words barely make it past my lips. The intense feelings gaining speed. Power.

"Why not?" He grunts, taking the shell of my ear between his teeth and nibbling me into an erratic state of need. His hard cock now rubbing against the seam of my ass and striking a different kind of fire in my belly. I want him to strip me down and ram into me. Fill me up and fuck me hard and raw. But that can't happen. It's Jaxon.

"Because it's wrong," I admit the truth, though, praying it doesn't sway him to stop, that he doesn't snap out of the sexual heat and come to his senses. Realize we're playing with fire. A fire so hot and scorching that I can't get past the thick of its smoke. I'm going to suffocate in its bliss. Get swallowed by its flames. Nothing has ever felt so good.

His fingers pinch down on my sensitive nub like he's trying to squeeze the pleasure right from the source. "Feels fucking right to me," he growls, scorching my neck with his lips. His tongue suctioning behind my ear, no doubt leaving a mark.

I push up onto my knees, needing to be closer. My fingers gripping his hair tighter. My back arching into his chest. My butt grinding down on his lap, while his fingers keep working their magic between my legs. I need him to fuck me.

"Jax…" I let the moan hang in the air, hoping he'll read my body's signs and rip my pants away; fill me with that massive thing that's dry fucking me into a tizzy.

"I know, baby," he groans, the thickness so heavy in his voice. "Know you need me to fuck you. But if I sink inside now, neither of us will last."

Exactly. So, what's the problem?

His other hand comes up, molding over my breast, tweaking my nipple as skillfully as he tweaks my clit. I cry out his name, realizing my mistake too late. Shit. Our parents are right downstairs and will hear us if I'm not careful. Fingers crossed our moms are in a boisterous giggle fit and they didn't just hear my wild sexual moan.

"You gotta keep it down, sexy girl, or the 'rents are gonna come up and put a stop to our fun." He bites down on the side of my neck and the jolting sting of pleasure surges right between my thighs. "Now, are you going to be a good girl so I can make you come?"

"Yes," I gasp, as he pinches my nipple harder, drenching my panties further.

"Good." He shifts behind me, pushing me back down onto all fours. "Bite down on your pillow, babe."

I do as I'm told, and just as I squeeze the plush material between my teeth, the hand he was squeezing my breast with slides down the back of my pants and two strong fingers plunge right inside my pussy. Like a surprise attack.

He pumps them inside, fucking me perfectly while his other hand never lets up on my swollen clit at the front. When his fingers hook forward, massaging a spot I didn't even know existed, I'm diving right into a sea of chaotic bliss. Screaming into my pillow as the tide of pleasure takes me under, drowning me in heat, tumbling me through a current of extreme need and rocking me with feelings I've never known. Jaxon consumes me whole and...he doesn't stop.

My body feels like the tide is taking me back out to sea. Like another wave is about to crest and I'm trying to swim like hell so I can catch it and ride it back to shore. Holy shit. This must be what they mean by multiple orgasms, because I'm still pulsing through aftershocks from my first one, yet building up again at the same time.

But just as the wave is about to crest at the top, about to peak, Jaxon's hands disappear from my body, and instead of getting doused with heat, I get flooded with ice-cold desperation. I let go of the pillow, about to plead for him to continue, but before the words leave my mouth, my pants are tugged down and his extra-thick, extra-long cock is pushing into me, filling me up from end to end.

Damn. Since when are high school guys equipped with such massive, heavy-duty equipment? With every thrust forward, every part of me is being massaged and rubbed to perfection. Who knew my massage was going to turn into a very thorough full-body massage? With multiple happy endings.

"Oh, fuck, Lex." His pained groan has me turning my head, wanting to see his face. His features are locked up tight. Eyes squeezed shut. Jaw clenched. Painful sweet bliss is taking him under. "You're so tight, baby. And so damn wet."

He's right about that. I've never had so much self-lube in my life. But Jaxon's turning me into a juicy fruit. With every thrust into me, the sounds get sloppier and sloppier, and the tightness in my lower belly gets heavier and heavier. I'm almost at the crest again, about to hit my breaking point. Ready to be rocked by another extreme orgasm. I thrust back to meet his hips and we slam together hard. A jolt of ecstasy blasts through me, and I bury my scream in my pillow.

"You need it harder, don't you?"

A desperate little whimper comes out with a nod. I want that big cock to fuck me until I can't walk right. Until I'm bruised in the most amazing way.

"Never imagined my little Lexie Lou wanted to be raw dogged rough and dirty." His mouth is back to my ear, his hot words sending a shiver down my spine. "You better bite down on that pillow again, because I'm about to shatter this tight little cunt."

Oh my God. Since when did my dear sweet friend develop such a dirty mouth? Jaxon's usually such a gentleman. Kind, sweet, polite. But right now, he's a filthy animal—and it's driving me crazy.

A smack lands on my butt and the sting sends a streak of fire straight between my legs, causing me to clench around his stiff shaft.

"Told you to bite that pillow. Now get it between those teeth so I can make you come. Otherwise, I'm going to have to pull out and shove my cock down your throat to keep you quiet. Dirty up that pretty face instead of this tight little hole."

Holy shit. This…this is what I've been craving. What I've needed. But the guys I dated could barely get me off with their fingers, let alone yield any power with their words. None of them had any control over my body, yet Jaxon is commanding my pleasure. It's like I'm a puppet and he's my master pulling my strings tighter and tighter with each passing second. Pretty soon, I'm going to snap and plummet into my orgasm.

But I'm not ready yet. I still want to be played with. To be toyed with. I glance back, defiance running through my veins. Curiosity pulsing at my clit. I want to see how far he'll go. How demanding he'll be. "You're gonna have to gag me, if you want me quiet, Jax."

CHAPTER 2

Jaxon

Oh, fuck! Since when did my sweet little Lexie Lou turn into such a dirty girl? I thrust into her hard, rutting up against her cervix. Her walls squeezing the cum right out of me. If I could have my way, I'd be making her scream my name. Make her beg for me to have mercy on this incredible pussy and give her the relief she's desperate for. But there's no way in hell I'm going to let our parents hear us and come and put a stop to this. Not after I'm finally getting what I want.

I shift back, yanking her upright, body flush against mine. My palm covering her mouth, my lips right by her ear. Another muffled whimper vibrates against my hand as my cock hits deeper. I slow my thrusts, savoring every second of this perfection, circling my hips and massaging her wet channel. Desperately fighting to hold my load at bay. My dick is feeling extra anxious, like I'm a virgin all over again. Only, my first time was nowhere near as incredible. Nor have any of my other sexual experiences come close to this.

"You always were so stubborn." I nip at her soft lobe, tugging her silky skin between my teeth, her pussy throbbing in response. God, she's amazing. Never have I ever felt free to be myself, to give into my true cravings. But with Lex, I can let down my guard. Let the fire burn through my veins. The dominant alpha that's been cuffed in social chains can finally come to the surface. The good boy everyone always expects me to be can be bad. And—she's melting for me, begging to be controlled, wanting to be tamed.

I give one more penetrating thrust, sheathing myself to the hilt before I'm pulling out. A moan of protest hits my palm, and her eyes go from half-lidded to wide open. I feel her pain, but my cock has to learn some patience. "If you want me back inside this little cunt"—I tighten my grip in her hair—"then you're going to have to beg my dick with that mouth of yours."

Her eyes flutter at my seething words, and she shifts to face me. I release my grip on her and sit back on my haunches. My hard, glistening cock standing proud, ready to be worshipped by those heart-shaped lips of hers. This is the moment I've played out in my mind as I've fisted my dick night after night. But I never imagined it would come to life.

I thought I was forever going to be stuck in the friend zone. I thought Lex saw me like a brother. After all, we've known each other since we were brought into this world. Born two days apart. Our parents having met in Lamaze class and becoming like family, raising their only children together. But as Lex lowers her head and her plump lips slide down my shaft, it's clear that she's right in the end zone with me, waiting to catch the winning touchdown. Both of us finally on the same playing field.

My cock hits the back of her throat and a groan slips out before I can bite it back. I'm just thankful I can hear laughter coming from downstairs; our moms are clearly already feeling the alcohol. Definitely don't want the dads coming up and interrupting the best blow job of my life. Never has any girl been able to deep throat me the way Lex is. She's taking almost all of me down, and what doesn't fit, she's fisting with a tight grip. Her other hand paying homage to my balls, cupping and teasing the cum right up to the tip.

I grab onto her hair, tugging her off before I explode. Her mouth is too good. But I'm not ready to come yet. I want to see how dirty she'll get. Want to know if there's a naughty little slut hiding beneath the princess cheerleader surface. She's a flawless beauty. Brown hair, chocolate brown eyes, killer body. Sweet. Smart. And has a heart of gold. But I want to know if under all that perfection there's a wildcat waiting to be set free.

I hold her tight, keeping her locked in place as I slide my cockhead over her lips. Her tongue comes out, swiping up the driblets of cum leaking from the top. The view before me is better than any I could've imagined. "You're jonesing for another taste, aren't you?"

She nods on a moan, those lips of hers parting. Tongue lapping lewdly as I stroke my sensitive skin all around her hungry mouth. "My dirty girl. So thirsty for it," I groan, smearing cum up the side of her cheek as she licks at the base of my cock. It's all so fucking incredible. The feelings beyond intense. The pleasure tacking up my spine, running all the way down to my toes. And soon, I'm going to blow.

Her arm slides between her legs, fingers trying to play with her clit. Obviously, she needs some relief, but jealousy roars down my shaft, tightening my balls. It's mine. That orgasm... Her pleasure... I'm the one who is going to give it to her. I'm the one who is going to make her come. Not her.

I grip her hair tighter, tilting her head back, forcing her eyes to lock on me. "You better drop that hand between your legs because the only one who's going to make that pussy quiver is me and this big fat cock." I press my dick against her lips, pushing past the seam of her mouth and sliding to the back of her throat.

17

Her eyes burn with stubborn fire. She's soaking up my need for control yet taunting me for more. When her hand stays wedged between her thighs, whimpered gasps panting against my shaft, forearm moving faster, I crack. I pull out of her perfect mouth, then I'm on her. Flipping her onto her back, spreading her thighs wide and slamming into her hot wet heat.

"You just couldn't be a good girl for me, could you? This thirsty little cunt just needed to be fucked." I pound into her hard. Fast. Her body rocking against the sheets. Perfect tits bouncing under her threadbare tank. She's worn the thing a thousand times, teased my raging hormones for years, and I tried to be a gentleman. Tried not to stare at her like a horny twerp. But today, I couldn't stop myself. She walked out of the closet, her pink nipple fully exposed at the top of her bra, and I couldn't turn away. Then, when she gave me that flirtatious wink, there was no holding back.

But I never expected her to feed my hunger. Never thought she'd pull her bra off, begging me to have a closer look. I thought she'd punch me in the arm and tell me to stop acting weird. But she didn't. And now, she's writhing beneath me. Her mouth buried against my forearm, muffled moans echoing around us as I fuck into her rough and raw.

I press two fingers to her clit, and as soon as I fiddle her swollen little bean, she's coming apart. Teeth sinking into my skin. Fingers digging into my hips. Pussy constricting me so tightly. And when I feel her warm juices dripping down my balls, I shatter. Coming at full force. Barely containing the roar that's lodged in my throat. God, it's too good. A wormhole of pleasure sucking me under as I drive in deeper.

I drop my head, biting the pillow between my teeth, finally releasing the bellow of lust bottled inside, savoring each and every blast of sparks as I slip and slide through her wet cunt. When my balls are milked dry, and my mind comes back into focus, I sit back up. Only to find my girl staring up at me with a look of awe in her eyes. I reach down between us, brushing my thumb over her perfect little bud, but she squirms beneath me, too sensitive to handle any more.

I take my cue and slide out, laying down beside her, struggling to catch my breath. My eyes close and our hot little session replays in my mind. My body is already revving back up when I'm suddenly being whacked in the head with her pillow. AGAIN.

"What the hell was that, Jax?" she practically shrieks. "God, we shouldn't have done that." She hits me again.

I grab the thing from her hand and toss it to the floor, wondering why on earth she's freaking out. What the hell just happened to my dirty girl whose body was begging for more just a minute ago? Whose teeth marks are still impressed upon my skin. She's acting like we just committed a crime. She's actually mad.

"Why the hell not?" I sit up and face her.

"Because our friendship is doomed now."

She climbs from the bed, pulling up her pants, looking completely frazzled. Maybe I should pin her against the wall and fuck her again, get her to calm the hell down.

Doomed? The way I see it, our relationship just got a hell of a lot better. I'm done sitting in the friend zone, waiting on the sidelines. I want to be her boyfriend. The man in her life. Her future fucking everything. And I don't understand why she didn't figure that out when I was ramming her with my cock. What did she think just happened between us? That we had some kind of fluke connection? Some kind of friends-with-benefits moment?

Let me tell you. This was definitely not some one-off fuck for me. Ever since I broke up with Jill last summer, I've known that Lex is the one I want to be with—for the rest of my life. It hit me like a lightning strike. One too many shit dates, and the big ol' question of what I was looking for in a partner lingering in my head, and the answer hit me dead-on. The one person in this world I love to spend time with is Lex. The only girl who's ever gotten me and made me feel special is Lex.

She makes me laugh. She's easy to talk to. And even when we're doing absolutely nothing, it's fun. Not to mention the fact that she's the most striking girl I've ever seen. Puberty didn't just do her justice; it blew her out of the realm of beautiful. So, there's no denying that my attraction for her was ever in question. And after what just happened between us, our chemistry is off the charts.

But even after an explosive, life-altering orgasm, she's still keeping me on the bench. What the hell?

"Why is it doomed, Lex?"

"Because..." She puts her hands on her hips, looking even more frustrated. "Now, we're going to be thinking about sex every time we're hanging out together. It's going to be awkward. Especially when one of us starts dating someone."

The fuck? Why is she acting like what just happened between us meant *nothing*? And *dating someone*? Is she interested in someone that I don't know about? Last I heard, she wasn't going to waste any more time on the guys at our school, which I was hoping this moment would've convinced her that there is only one guy worth her time. But from the way she's talking, it sounds like she already has someone else in mind.

"Why? You got a thing for someone?"

I'm trying to keep my cool, but jealousy is rolling up my nerves, wrapping around my heart and squeezing.

"No." She shakes her head. "But that could change."

Wow. Talk about a punch to the gut. She's not even considering me as an option. Like it's not even registering that what we have and what we just shared was amazing. Not just amazing, it was freaking incredible. But it's like she doesn't even fucking see it.

Apparently, what just happened between us was a moment

of sexual weakness for her. After all, I was the one who initiated things. She warned me from the beginning that we shouldn't do this. But then I made it to where her body couldn't resist. So now what the fuck do I do? How the hell do I convince her to want me? How do I get myself out of this damn friend zone?

Knock. Knock. The tap on the door has us both turning. My shoulders tense when I hear her dad's voice.

"Hey, you two. Just wanted to let you know that your folks are heading out, Jax. Your dad's taking your mom out to the car."

In other words, Mom has had too much wine, and Dad needs to get her home before she passes out.

Lex turns to me, looking panicked. "Do you think he heard?" she mouths.

I shake my head and point to the TV. The movie we have on is loud enough to cover our voices. And ironically, the actors sound like they're having the same argument we were just having.

She rushes into her closet, leaving me to deal with her dad. I stand up, making sure my dick is tucked back into my joggers and check for any cum smears on my pants. As soon as I'm in the clear, I go to open the door, wondering why he didn't just barge right in. It's not like it was locked, though it should've been.

"So, who won the game?" I ask, trying to sound casual as I come face to face with the father of the girl I just fucked hot and dirty. A man who's practically an uncle to me.

He rolls his eyes, shaking his head. "They did. But next time, we'll take them down."

I chuckle at that and then turn toward Lex who's coming out of her closet wearing a big baggy sweatshirt. Making the grungy thing look like lingerie. "I'll see you at school tomorrow," I tell her, clearing my throat to hide the lust in my voice.

"Sounds good." She smiles. "And don't watch the rest of the movie without me."

"I won't." I smirk, playing along.

I didn't see a single second of the thing. All I saw was Lexie's beautiful body unwinding under my touch. Her hips squirming when I started kneading her perfect rear end. Then the dark patch of damp material between her thighs, letting me know exactly what was on her mind. And that's when I decided to take the plunge. To give into temptation once and for all.

"Night, Mr. Grayson. Thanks for dinner." I tip my head as I walk past him.

I quickly make my way downstairs and out to my dad's car before the boner trying to rise in my pants draws any attention. I climb into the back seat and Mom lets out a loud hiccup then starts giggling at herself. Man, she's a lightweight. She probably only had one glass of wine and she's toast.

"Let's get her home." My dad shakes his head, chuckling as he pulls out of the drive.

"You kids have fun?" mom asks, hiccuping again and bursting into another fit of laughter.

"Yep." I was having a lot of fun. The best night of my life, actually. All the way up until the point where Lex shot me down. What I want to know is why she's not even considering the possibility of us being a couple. We obviously get along well since we're best friends. And now we know the chemistry between us is off the freaking chain. So why couldn't things work?

I think it's time for me and Lex to have a serious talk. But we're not doing it over the phone. I want to see her face and gauge her reaction when I tell her that I'm in love with her. I want to see the look in those brown eyes when I tell her I want to have a future with her, one that leads us down the aisle and with my baby in her belly. She's never been able to hide her true feelings from me, so I won't be discussing this matter until we're face to face.

So now, I need to find a time for us to do that. I pull out my phone and shoot her a text.

Me: You wanna hang out tomorrow night? Dinner and a movie? I know you've been wanting to see *Deviant Behavior*.

The movie is just a way to tempt her into agreeing since she's been asking me to see it since it hit the theaters. But I'm hoping our dinner conversation goes well, and that we'll be driving up to the bluff instead, having a repeat of tonight.

Lexie Lou: Sure. We should stop by the Halloween store first so we can get what we need for your party.

As long as I can get her alone, I'll agree to anything. I'm just thankful she's not turning me down, acting awkward and shying away from me.

Me: Sounds like a plan.

Lexie Lou: So, we're good???

Tension stiffens my jaw. She wants to make sure our "friend-ship" is perfectly intact. But as far as I'm concerned, we're no longer just best friends, we're going to be everything.

Me: Yes, we're good, Lex. Always.

Tonight, I'll play the game, placate my flustered girl. Let her nerves settle and the chemical reaction saturate. But come tomorrow, it's going to be my mission to get her on the same page. To prove that we're right for each other. Because nothing is ever going to come close to what we have together. I know the fire will never burn this hot with anyone else.

CHAPTER 3

Lexie

I can't stop thinking about him. Everything that happened last night keeps replaying in my mind, sending my body into a tailspin as I think about how domineering Jax was. I've seen him take charge on the football field, watched him dominate the game with his teammates, but when it comes to me and our friendship, he's always been so calm and obliging. Sweet and cuddly. A gentleman through and through. But last night, he took charge of my body and dominated my pleasure.

I turn the corner and my stomach does a back flip when I see Jax waiting for me by my locker. This is exactly what I was afraid of. He's waited for me every day since middle school, yet it feels different now. Especially since I'm checking him out. And man, does he look good today. His muscles fill out his button-down shirt perfectly. Jeans hugging his thick thighs. And he's got a backwards baseball cap on, which is seriously one of the sexiest looks on a guy. And the sexy smirk he's giving me has my body already feeling flushed.

How the heck am I supposed to act normal and pretend like

nothing happened between us when he's looking at me like that?

"Hey, gorgeous."

His eyes travel down my frame, and my stomach goes haywire with flutters. Now, I'm even more flustered. "None of that," I snap, turning to open my locker, wanting to bury my head inside and hide my rosy cheeks.

"What?" His hot breath casts over my ear, hard body pressing against my side, dousing me in flames. "I'm not allowed to tell my sexy little Lex how fine she looks in that short plaid skirt? You look like a dirty little schoolgirl who's in need of a good spanking from the principal."

"Jaxon Miller," I sigh, struggling to keep my legs from wobbling. "You can't say things…" My breathless groan dies on my tongue as I hear Ava's voice.

"Hey, guys!"

I look over my shoulder and force a smile at my dear friend as she comes walking up to my side.

"Hey, girl!" I lean in for a hug, thankful for her perfect timing, because apparently, Jaxon and I need a chaperone right now.

I knew this was going to happen. That sex would constantly be on the brain anytime we're together. Dammit. We totally messed up. And as soon as he finds himself a girlfriend, I'm going to be totally jealous and miserable.

I grab my books and close my locker a little too hard. "You ready for the quiz today?" I ask her, shoving all the craziness to the back of my brain as I shove my books inside my bag.

"Yep. I studied while I was babysitting last night."

I'm not surprised. Ava's always babysitting. She's practically the McGavins live-in nanny.

"Hey, Jax." She looks up at the guy whose eyes are still burning me up with their stare. "Is there a theme for the Fright

Bash? I'm going shopping after school for a costume and need some guidance."

"So are we," I chime in. "Jax and I are going to the Halloween store after school. Do you want to come?"

I sneak a side glance in his direction, hoping he's not picking up on the fact that I need a wingman to make sure I can handle myself around him and not do anything else that may jeopardize our friendship. He, too, needs a chaperone so his mouth doesn't get us into any more trouble.

"Sure!" She smiles. "That'd be awesome."

"Great. I'll shoot a text to the girls and see if anyone else wants to join. Hey, Jax..." Another heatwave hits when I meet his eyes. *Man, I'm in so much trouble.* "Do you want to ask the guys to come too?"

"Um...Yeah... Sure. But I think most of the guys will be working at the Fright House tonight." It doesn't sound like he's too thrilled by the idea of our friends joining, which sends me into another tizzy.

"Right." I nod, my stomach feeling like a swarm of bees have now formed a hive in the pit. "Well, Ava and I have to get to class so we can quiz each other real quick, but I'll see you at lunch." I lean in to give him a hug like usual, but it doesn't feel the same. Everything is awkward between us now.

Man, this is so not good. If the weirdness between us doesn't fade fast, our friendship is going to be toast. And I can't lose my best friend. He's my rock. My ride or die. When girl drama ensues or I'm having a bad day, he's the one I can turn to to make it all better. He's the one who can talk me down from any emotional ledge and help me fix my problems.

But, right now, my problem is him, and he can't fix the way I feel. The only thing that will fix it, is time— and the fading memory of what we did. Although, I doubt I'm ever going to forget the hottest sexual experience of my life.

"Good luck on your quiz." His voice rumbles over me, and I

jerk back, realizing I was still wrapped around him, practically nuzzling into his hard muscles. Shit. I need to get my act together and get my head out of the gutter.

I quickly utter thanks, and grab Ava's arm, wanting to get to class and away from the guy with the sexy smirk on his face ASAP.

"So, *is* there a theme for the party?" Ava asks as we start heading down the hall.

I shake my head, trying to brush off the flustering thoughts nagging at my nerves. "Not this year. So you can dress up however you want."

We walk into class and take our seats. I plop my bag down and pull out my phone, wondering if I should text Jaxon and tell him that he needs to behave. There's no way in hell I can do the friends-with-benefits thing. I know myself. My heart and mind have a tendency to go all in. I'm looking for long-lasting love, and that's clearly not what Jax wants. Otherwise, he would've kissed me last night when we had sex. Or even after, but he didn't. He laid down next to me, saying and doing nothing.

Because what was there to say? He got what he wanted and was done.

My stomach tightens at the thought and I start typing up a text to the girls instead, deciding it's better not to make things any more awkward with Jax.

Me: Hey, girls! Ava, Jax, and I are going to the Halloween store after school and then we're going to grab dinner and see *Deviant Behavior*. Anyone else want to join?

"We're going to dinner and the movies, too?" Ava asks, popping her head up from her phone.

"Yeah, that's the plan, if you're up for it?"

"Sure!" She nods. "I'm up for anything. I haven't had a night off from babysitting in forever."

Yeah, I know. We barely get to see her anymore.

My phone dings in with responses from the others and I

look down, hoping we'll get the whole group out tonight. When it comes to my feelings for Jax, there's definitely going to be safety in numbers.

Mercy: I wish. But I have family bible study tonight.

Even if that weren't the case, I don't think Mercy would even want to see the movie with us. It's rated mature and probably way too racy for my sweet virginal friend.

Piper: Sorry, have to pass. Cord and I are having a family night in.

I roll my eyes. In other words, she and her stepbrother are having a date night. I don't understand why they don't just come out with their relationship already. It's not like it's a secret that they both have feelings for each other. Just look at the way they kiss on each other all the time and practically make out in the hall. They aren't hiding a thing. And who cares anyway. No one thinks it's weird. In fact, I think their taboo relationship is hot.

Sam: I can't make it. I have dance tonight. But you'll definitely have to let me know how the movie is. I'm dying to see it.

Me: LAME! Fine, we'll just go without you. But I expect you all to go to the Fright House this Friday.

"Oh, yay," Ava cheers. "I've been dying to go, and I actually have the night off. The McGavins are taking Lilly out of town this weekend, which means I'm free."

"Sweet!" I give her a high five.

Piper: What??? No!!!! You guys know I don't like scary things.

I roll my eyes again. That's exactly the response I expected. It's okay though. I have all week to work on changing her mind, and I'll get the other girls to help too.

Sam: I'm in! I've been wanting to check it out. And Piper will be there too ;)

Mercy: Count me in!

Me: Awesome! See you girls at lunch.

I tuck my phone away and turn toward Ava. "Looks like it's just going to be the three of us tonight. Unless any of the guys join."

She nods. "You ready to study now?"

"Yep." I lean over to grab my book out of my bag, and Ava suddenly lets out a gasp.

"Is everything okay, Ave?" I look over and see her shoving a yellow piece of paper into the bottom of her bag. She bobs her head, yes, but the nervous look in her eyes doesn't agree.

"Yeah. Just...um...realized I forgot to study a certain section last night. Can we review chapter 11 first?" She sits up and quickly opens her book, frantically flipping to the section.

For some reason, I feel like she's lying to me and that whatever's got her jumpy has to do with the note she frantically hid away, but I also know that Ava is a stickler when it comes to her grades and her perfect GPA, so I could be wrong. All I know is, right now, I could definitely use another review of the material because my mind was a bit scattered last night.

CHAPTER 4

Jaxon

"Mr. Miller, you need to see me after class."

Mrs. Jansen places my test down on my desk and the big "D" in the corner circled in red is blaring at me. This is my second one this semester, which means my grade is seriously hurting, and I'm going to fail if I don't get my act together. As soon as the last student has left the room, I take my walk of shame to her desk, already knowing exactly what she's going to say.

"Jaxon, that's the second test you've failed this grading cycle." She shoves her glasses up the bridge of her nose, looking as equally disappointed as she sounds. "I hate to say this, but if you don't have a passing grade for this grading cycle, I'll be forced to inform Coach Rally and will be requesting your suspension from the team until you prove that football is not interfering with your academics."

Is she fucking kidding me? We're about to make the finals. For the first time in ten years, the school has a chance to head to the state championship. There's no way I'm sitting on the sidelines while my teammates take home that trophy. Besides, they need me out there. I'm the best wide receiver we've got.

"Now, I'm a fair teacher, Mr. Miller, and I know how much football means to you and how much you mean to the team, so I'm going to give you a chance to pull up your grade. I'll let you retake this test during study hall tomorrow. You also have the paper due on Friday, and if you do well on both, you'll be in the clear."

"Thank you, Mrs. Jansen." Relief unwinds my stomach. "I appreciate the chance, and I'm not going to fail again." I'm going to study my ass off tonight and then turn in the best damn paper on "Religion in the Modern World" she's ever seen. But that means I won't be able to make it out with the girls tonight. Not that it really matters; Lex barely spoke to me at lunch. And clearly, she has no interest in being alone with me since she invited the girls to join us.

"Okay, well, run along." She dismisses me. "I don't want you to be late for practice." I nod, thanking her again and dart out the door, nearly bumping right into someone as I turn down the hall.

"Sorry," I say, righting us both, realizing it's Sienna Rushmont I almost took down— my least favorite person in this school. I scoot around her and keep heading toward the locker room. If I'm late, Coach will make me run stadiums, and that's the last thing I want to do.

* * *

"HEY, LEX," I call out, stopping her right before she heads into the girls' locker room. Man, she's sexy in her sports bra and shorts, sweat glistening on her skin. I grip my helmet tighter, fighting the urge not to toss her over my shoulder and carry her into the locker room with me. I'd take her straight into the shower, lather her up, and get her all nice and dirty. Then I'd push her down to her knees and make her give my pipes a good cleaning. Damn, I'm still dreaming of that perfect mouth and how her throat took me so deep.

"What's up?" She asks, her shoulders tensing as I step up to her.

This is exactly what I'm talking about. She doesn't even want to be around me anymore. All day she's been uncomfortable in my presence. She'll probably be relieved I'm bowing out on our plans tonight.

"I'm not gonna be able to make it out tonight. I failed another test in World History and Mrs. Jansen's giving me a chance to retake it tomorrow. She said if I don't pass, she's telling Coach to suspend me from the team."

"No," she gasps. "She can't do that. They need you on that field, Jax."

I know they do. Our second-string receiver has a broken ankle, which means Coach would be putting in Manny. And that kid misses 80 percent of the time.

"Okay, well, do you need any help studying? I can take a rain check with Ava and help quiz you on the material."

As much as I'd love to take her up on that offer, she'd be too much of a distraction. She was right with her assessment: there's one dominant thought when I'm in her presence and it's how I want to get her back under me. My mouth buried between her legs. Her wet little pussy coming apart on my tongue. So, *no*, I can't let her be my study partner tonight.

"Nah, I have an easier time focusing when I study by myself. Besides, I don't want to screw up your plans with Ava."

The fact that she even offered to help me has the tension loosening a bit. At least she's willing to be alone with me. I'll take that as a good sign. A steppingstone to getting what I want.

"All right, well, I'll send you pics of the new dolls they have at the Halloween store, and you can let me know if there's anything you want me to get for the Fright Bash."

"Thanks, Lexie Lou. Sorry to bail on our plans."

She shakes her head, finally seeming like her usual self. "That's okay. I understand. You can make it up to me later."

I nearly groan at her comment. I'd love to make it up to her later. I'd spend hours apologizing with my mouth and tongue, worshipping every inch of her body. I'd grovel until she's begging for a reprieve.

I step forward, removing the space between us, reaching out and running my fingers along the waistband of her shorts. "You should text me when you two are done with the movies. I may be finished studying and be able to make it up to you then." I dip my fingers lower, teasing my way under the material.

The heat hits her eyes and her cheeks, but then suddenly freezes over as she grabs onto my hand and stops me from seeking what I want.

"I meant we can go to dinner and a movie some other time," she growls, moving out of my reach. "You have to stop, Jax. You're making things worse."

Making things worse? What the hell does she mean by that? And why is she fighting this so hard? The attraction is undeniable. It's like blue fire, a flame so hot it leaves you scarred. And I know by how hard her nipples are and the way she's squeezing her thighs together, not to mention how hard she squirted for me last night, that she feels it too.

I seriously need to get to the bottom of this stronghold stance, but I can't right now. The last thing I need before I go study is her rejection sitting heavy on my heart and weighing down my concentration. Which means, our little heart-to-heart will have to wait.

"Where are you guys going to dinner?" I ask, trying to get back to neutral ground, ignoring her comment and the dejected feeling sinking in.

"Tucci's. Which reminds me, I have to run. Ava's waiting on

me. We're trying to pack it all in so we can make the eight o'clock showing."

She quickly darts into the girls' locker room before I can get another word out, and I'm left staring at the closed door, wishing I could go in after her and press her up against the lockers. Prove just how incredible things are between us. I'd give her body exactly what I know it needs: a good firm hand and a hard fuck. But if I'm caught inside the girls' locker room, I won't just be suspended from the team, I'll be kicked off and suspended from school.

"Hey, Jaxon." I turn toward the voice calling for me, surprised when I see Sienna Rushmont approaching. Wonder if she came to bitch me out for running into her earlier.

"What's up?" I ask, my voice lacking all patience for the girl whose jealousy toward Lex knows no bounds.

"I couldn't help but overhear what Mrs. Jansen said to you after class."

Awesome, so now the whole damn school is going to know I'm failing and about to get benched. The guys are going to reem my ass out if they think their chance at state is in jeopardy, and that's the last thing I need right now.

"Yeah, and your point?"

"I just wanted to tell you that I missed the first test and had to take her make-up exam. I haven't gotten it back yet, so I'm guessing she'll give you the same version tomorrow. Anyway, I just wanted to offer my help. I think I remember most of the questions, and if we go through the book together, I think it will trigger anything I've forgotten."

I'm not sure why she's offering to help me, nor am I sure I want her help. But bottom line is, I need to ace this test tomorrow, so whether I want to spend time with Sienna or not is irrelevant. What's important is not letting my team down. Besides, after all the shit this girl has caused, it's about time she actually did a bit of good. Not that helping me ace the test will redeem her by any means. But I can use all the help I can get.

"Is there a catch, Sienna?" I cross my arms, wondering why she's willing to help her enemy's best friend. A guy who's never given her a friendly look or made one nice comment about her. Ever. Seems a little fishy to me.

"Um...kind of." And here we go. The little witch wants something in return. "I was hoping for an invite to your Halloween party. All my friends are going, and I hate being left out of the fun. Especially since it's our senior year."

She's never been invited to the Fright Bash before because Lex is my one and only priority and I didn't want to put my best friend in a position where she had to come face to face with her nemesis. I still don't like the idea, but the party is going to be so big, the two of them may never cross paths. And even if they do, Lex will assume Sienna invited herself. Which is technically what she's doing.

"Yeah, sure," I concede. "But I don't want any issues between you and Lex. If you cause any problems, you're out, Sienna."

She shakes her head. "No. I promise there won't be a problem. We're all heading off to college next year and I'm hoping we can put the past behind us. I'll even wear a mask so she won't know I'm there."

Wow. I'm shocked by her surprisingly mature response. Maybe this invite will keep things smooth between the girls for the rest of the school year. It'd be nice for things to finally be drama free.

"How much time have you got to review with me? I need to run into the locker room and shower."

"I have all night." She smiles. "You go get cleaned up and I'll be waiting on the bleachers."

CHAPTER 5

Lexie

"Sorry, ladies. I can seat you now, but it's over an hour wait on food. We have too many takeout orders and the ovens are backed up."

I turn toward Ava. "We won't make the movie. I think we should go somewhere else."

"I agree." She nods.

We both turn and thank the hostess before heading right back out the doors we just came through. "Okay, so now where should we eat?" I ask, bummed I'm not going to have my chicken parm fix. It's my go-to comfort food, and with all the crazy thoughts running through my head, I could definitely use some comfort.

"You want to go to the diner? I've been dieting all week and could totally go for a burger and a milkshake."

"Why on earth are you on a diet, Ava? Your body is killer."

What the heck is she smoking? Curves are in. And hers are amazing. I'd give anything to have an ass like hers. She doesn't even work on it and has the kind of peach girls envy.

"I'm trying to lose fifteen pounds so that when I get to college and gain the 'freshman fifteen' it will all even out."

I shake my head at her ridiculousness. "Come on, crazy girl. Let's go get you a greasy burger then."

I usually never eat at the diner. Ever since I got sick from their pancakes, I've had a bad association with the place. But for my good friend who never gets a night off from babysitting and who has been deprived all week of yummy food, I'll deal with my aversion. Besides, a burger actually sounds good.

"So, what are the McGavins going to do without you next year?" I ask, pulling back onto Main Street and heading toward the diner. Thankfully, it's closer to the movie theater so we'll be good on time.

"I think they'll hire a full-time nanny, especially since Rye and Mason will be gone too."

I still shake my head every time I think about the guys' situation. It's seriously messed up how everything went down with their parents. But on the plus side, now the two best friends are stepbrothers.

"Where do Rye and Mase want to go to school?"

"I don't know." She shrugs. "They're never home. And when they are, they never talk to me."

The hint of disappointment in her voice has me turning my head. Once upon a time Ava had a crush on Rye, but I thought she was long over it. Out of the two stepbrothers, he's the grumpy one, and Mason is the friendly, outgoing one. Both equally good-looking. And both equally unattainable to the girls at our school. In fact, I heard they only date college girls.

I turn my attention back on the road, deciding not to press her about it. Even if she does have a thing for Rye, it's never going to happen. Not if the rumors are true.

"Well, I'd put money on them both going to the same college," I state. "Those two are inseparable." *Just like me and Jax.*

God, just thinking his name has my body heating. I'm not

sure what's going on with him, or between us, but he's still not letting up with his flirtations and it's driving my body crazy. But I don't understand his motive. I'm not sure if it's because we just had a seriously hot moment together and he wants a repeat, or if he's like Justin Timberlake in the movie *Friends with Benefits* and wants some kind of no-strings-attached arrangement.

Since college is right around the corner, he may not see the point in getting involved in a relationship and just want some easy "fun." The only problem is my heart's already struggling with our one moment. There's no way I'd be able to do a casual thing with him.

"Yeah, but they may get drafted by different teams, so who knows." She pulls me back from the deep end of my thoughts. "What about you and Jaxon? What are you going to do next year while he's at state and you're at Michigan?"

This is another reason why a relationship between us would never work. We're going to be halfway across the country from each other, and long-distance is like a death sentence to a couple. And once we broke up, our friendship wouldn't be the same. It's not like we could just snap our fingers and go back to being best friends again. My heart would be hurting too much. My body would definitely be suffering from the loss. And I'd never want to know about his dating life. It would destroy me.

Which is exactly why we have to put a stop to the craziness NOW.

"I'm going to miss him." My stomach drops at the thought. "But we'll both be busy. And I'm sure we'll talk every day on the phone."

"Can I ask you a question?"

I pull into a parking spot and shut the car off. "Sure. You can always ask me anything."

"How come you two never dated?"

That's apparently the question of the hour. "I don't know." I shrug. "We've just always been best friends. Like brother and sister. I think we were just so close in that way that we never thought about each other in the other way."

At least, that was the case up until last night. Now, it's all I can think about. It's like I can't even see Jaxon as my good buddy who used to give me wet willies all the time. Now, all I see is the dominant alpha who has the most amazing willy and gave me the most incredible orgasms of my life.

"And what we have is so special"— I stop myself from sinking further into forbidden territory— "that I don't think either one of us wants to chance losing it."

Which is why I need to stop having these inappropriate thoughts, and why I need to tell Jaxon to stop trying to get into my pants. But it'll have to wait until tomorrow because he's home studying for his test and I don't want to distract him. He'll be absolutely devastated if he can't be in the playoff game. It's what he's worked so hard for. All these years have led up to this one moment.

"Yeah, I can appreciate that." She smiles.

We both climb out of the car and I hit the lock button on my key fob, walking up to the entrance. Ava holds the door open for me and I thank her as I enter. As soon as I see who's sitting in the booth on the right, I almost turn around and walk right back out. I can't believe on the one and only night I decide to eat here the one person I despise is here too. Now, I'm going to have an even worse aversion to this place.

Sienna's eyes dart to mine as if sensing my arrival. Her smile turns into an evil sneer just like it always does when I enter a room. I'm not sure what I ever did to her or why she hates me so much, especially now when she's gotten what she wanted— me gone from the studio and her in the lead—but she goes out of her way to let me know that I'm the bane of her existence. Between her attitude, the rumors she tries to spread, and her failed attempts of trying to turn my cheer squad against me, it's clear that the hatred still burns hot in her blood.

"Besides dance, Sie, what are you into? What do you do for fun?"

The deep male voice, the one I've heard all my life, has me finally looking toward the person sitting in the booth with her. My stomach tightens and the air in my lungs refuses to release. Why is Jaxon here? And why is he with her? And why does it sound like they're on a date?

"Ladies, would you like a table or a booth?" the waitress asks, but her question goes ignored. All I can hear is the pounding of my heart. All I care about is why Jaxon is here with the witch. He said he had to study tonight. He canceled plans with me, claiming he needed to be home preparing for his test tomorrow. But he's not home. He's here with the bitch. He lied.

My feet take me closer, as if needing to have a look at the front of his face. Hoping that by some miracle I'm wrong. That maybe my eyes and ears are deceiving me. Maybe my obsessed thoughts have created a mirage.

"I love coming to the football games and watching *you*." Sienna smiles, her sultry voice pricking up my nerves like needles. She's trying to seduce him. It's obvious in her eyes exactly what she wants. "You're so incredible, Jax."

The sound of his name nearly has me locking in place. It's undeniably him. My best friend is on a date with my bully.

"Thanks," he says, his voice gentle, sweet. Not a shred of hatred or disgust toward the girl in the smoothness of it. "And thanks again for tonight and for keeping this our little secret."

Little secret?

There's only one reason he'd want to keep their date a secret. He didn't want me finding out about it.

Sienna reaches her hand out, running her sharp, red-painted claws up his forearm. "It's my pleasure. I'm more than happy to help you with your *problem*. And I promise this will stay between us. I completely understand why you want us to be discreet."

Problem? Is she talking about the hard-on I left him with outside of the locker room because that's what it sure sounds like.

Her eyes snap to mine, triumph swimming in her glare. She thinks she won. That she's finally struck me down by stealing my best friend away from me. She has. I've never been cut so deep. Felt a pain so bad. Jealousy is pouring in, like I'm being waterboarded by the emotion. But betrayal, anger, disappointment, and pure utter devastation take me under.

I'd expect a move like this from Sienna. I'm actually surprised it took her so long to go after the one thing I care about the most in this world. But Jax... I never expected him to betray me like this. He knows what she's like, knows what she's done. He hated her just as much as I do. Or so he said. *Just like he said he had to study tonight.*

"You okay, Lex?" Ava's whispered voice is like a life preserver. I lean into the sound and get myself to turn in her direction.

Right as I grab hold of my sanity, I hear the witch's voice, "Hey, Ava! Not babysitting tonight?"

"Does it look like I'm babysitting?" my dear friend answers, rolling her eyes at the stupid question. She doesn't like Sienna either. Not just because Ava's a loyal friend and she knows what the witch did to me, but because she knows exactly what kind of person Sienna is. Conniving, backstabbing, and pure evil.

"Lex?"

Jaxon's voice nearly takes me to the floor, but somehow, I manage to find the strength and push back the pain; all my years as a cheerleader coming to my rescue. No matter what, I will never let her know she's destroyed me.

I turn with a perfect smile on my face. "Hey, Jax. Fancy seeing you two here." He probably chose to bring her here because never in a million years would he think I'd be here. "Did you get your studying done?"

He swallows hard. I guess that's a no. And here, I was worried that sex was going to destroy our friendship. Who knew it was going to be Sienna Rushmont that ruined us.

"We're just taking a break and having some dinner, but I definitely feel better about the material already." Interesting. I thought he couldn't study with anybody. Another lie to keep me from finding out who he really wanted to spend his time with. And to make things worse, he's acting like everything is normal. Like it's not totally fucked up that he's with the girl who's bullied me for years.

"You're going to ace it," Sienna chimes in, batting her eyes at him like a moron, her claws still clinging to his forearm. "I'll stay up all night with you. My parents are out of town so you can totally crash in my bed. They'll never know."

My chest constricts. My stomach plummeting into the pit of despair. I'm not sure I can keep up the act any longer. It hurts too much. Jaxon's going to spend the night at her house. "Sleep" in her bed. When just last night he was fucking me in mine.

"Hey, Lex. Are you good if we grab candy at the movie instead of getting dessert here? I'm suddenly having a major craving for Raisinets."

I turn my attention toward Ava and see it in her eyes. She's saving me. Throwing out the life preserver again for me to grab onto. And I do.

"Yeah, sure." I smile, trying so hard to hold on with my slippery emotions. "I actually could totally go for some Skittles." I look back toward Jax, refusing to give the witch the satisfaction. "We're going to take off, but good luck with the studying."

I follow Ava out of the restaurant, counting backwards from a hundred. Keeping my feet steady, one in front of the other. "Give me your keys," Ava says, as soon as we're outside. I take them from my pocket and hand them over. I follow her to my car and slide into the passenger seat. Waiting until the moment we're out of any possible view to let the tears run freely.

42

CHAPTER 6

Jaxon

Fuck. What the hell was she doing here? Lex hates the diner. Ever since we were kids and she threw up their pancakes, she's never been able to stomach the place. I thought for certain I'd be in the clear, that she'd never know about my study date with Sienna. But I was wrong. And now...I'm screwed.

"Excuse me for a sec, Sienna. I just need to run to the bathroom."

"No, problem. But it's Sie, remember?" She rolls her eyes. "Sienna is just so formal, Jax."

I keep *my* eyes from rolling, tipping my head before turning and heading to the restroom. As soon as I'm out of eyeshot, I'm dialing Lex's number. One ring and it gets sent straight to voicemail. Fuck. She's icing me out. This is what I was worried about. Why I chose the damn diner in the first place.

The burger I just wolfed down is now starting to feel like a congealed greasy weight of dread in my stomach. I knew the smile on Lexie's face was just for Sienna's sake. She thinks I'm a traitor. But she doesn't know why I'm here. She needs to let me explain.

Me: It's not what it looks like, Lex. Sienna took the make-up exam and offered to help me study since she knows all the questions. I promise I haven't turned to the dark side ;)

I'm wondering if she's going to ignore my text too, but then I see the three little dots scrolling on the screen, and I'm holding my breath for her response to come through.

Lexie Lou: That's awfully nice of her to help you. Hope you pass the test. Have to turn my phone off now.

Relief puts the air back inside my lungs and has my shoulders slackening. Thank God she understands and isn't throwing me her stubborn sass. I was definitely worried there for a sec that I was going to be digging my way out of the doghouse, but I was wrong. She understands how much football means to me and that I can't let my team down. That's the only reason I'd ever find myself being nice to Sienna.

Me: Thanks for understanding, Lexie Lou. Enjoy the movie. Wish I was hanging with you girls instead.

She doesn't respond, but she's probably already inside the theater, glaring at people for texting during the previews. She hates seeing phones light up around the room. My Lex is a stickler when it comes to movies—another one of her spunky traits that I find adorable.

Man, I really wish I was there with her. Sitting next to her in that dark room. Taking her hand in mine. Pulling her into my body. Trying to see how far she'll let me misbehave.

Shit. Now, I'm hard, and if I go back out to the table like this, Sienna will think she's the reason for my excitement, and that's the last impression I intend to give. The girl may be considered pretty by popular opinion, but her personality makes her ugly in my eyes. Now, my Lex, on the other hand, she's not only beautiful on the outside, but she's stunning on the inside. Her beauty runs soul deep.

I lock myself inside the stall, then slip my hand down the front of my pants, giving my cock a good squeeze. My mind goes straight to yesterday as I start tugging myself in a firm grip. The vision of my sexy Lex on all fours, letting me finger fuck that tight hole of hers. Her need growing desperate as she practically moaned for my dick to fill her up and take her rough and raw. Then the way she squirted against my shaft as I let the beast come to the surface and stake his claim. She craved my dominance and wanted more. And I'm pretty sure I could've gone a hell of a lot further and that pussy would've purred like a kitten.

The image of me putting a leather collar around her neck comes to the forefront of my mind, fueling my lust deeper. It's a fantasy I've played out when I'm alone in bed. Her wearing a heart-shaped little silver tag that tells the world who she belongs to. Me, ordering her to behave. Finding discreet ways to make her obey me in public, and maybe some non-discreet ways too.

After our little encounter earlier, I fantasized about carrying her into the boys' locker room and shoving her up against the wall. I'd rip her bra down and let the guys see how incredible my baby's tits are. Then I'd hike up that little cheerleader skirt and fuck her to the grunts and growls of my envious teammates. And when I'm done marking her insides with my cum, showing everyone exactly who owns her pussy, I'd carry her straight into the shower and worship every inch of her body while my name falls from her lips for everyone to hear. Coach would be so fucking turned on, he wouldn't even write me up for it.

The cum goes spewing into the toilet and I bite down on my fist, trying to keep myself from roaring as the explosion hits. Damn. Even my Fantasy Lexie is incredible. She's a good, wicked little girl who does as her master says and loves every minute of it.

Man, I wish I didn't have this test looming over my head, because I'd be running into the movie theater and dragging Lex out so we can have the "talk" tonight.

CHAPTER 7

Lexie

"Girls, can I get you any hot chocolate?" Ava's mom asks through the door. She saw my face when we came in and knows something's wrong. I'm just glad it's her and not my mom, because my mom would pry.

I shake my head, and Ava answers her, "No thanks, Mom. We're good."

"All right, well if you two need anything, just let me know. Oh, and Ava sweetie, you got some mail today. I put it on your desk."

Ava darts over to her desk, suddenly looking anxious, like she's expecting something important. But she picks up the envelopes and shoves them into her drawer without even looking through them. That's odd. But maybe none of it was what she was hoping for. Although, I'd be curious what the red envelope that looked like a greeting card is.

"Did he text you again?" She turns, looking almost flustered. Clearly, whatever she was expecting didn't come.

"No." I shake my head. But I'm not expecting another response from Jaxon. He thinks I'm in the movie right now based on what I wrote in my last text. I just wanted to end the conversation before we got into a huge fight. There's no way I'm going to be responsible for him failing his test tomorrow and being kicked off the team. I'd never forgive myself for that, and he'd forever resent me for it too. So I told him what I knew he needed to hear. But I'm far from okay with what he did.

If there was someone who had done awful things to him—a teammate who'd bullied him constantly, stole his position out from under him, and then did everything in their power to make the rest of his team hate him—I'd never in a million years spend time with that person. I don't care what was riding on the line for me, I would never make nice with the enemy and betray my best friend like that.

Not only that, but it didn't seem like just an innocent study date to me. He was asking her get-to-know-you questions. He already gave her a cute nickname, calling her Sie. And...he did nothing to remove her hand from his body when she was running her fingers up and down his arm, teasing his skin with her sharp nails. It was like he was soaking up the attention, inviting more. And Sienna was eating it up. From the look on her face, she definitely had more than world history on the brain.

Back when we were friends, she had told me she had the biggest crush on Jaxon and was hoping he'd ask her to the Fright Ball. Considering Jax has only gotten hotter over the years, I'm sure that crush has only grown. Well...it looks like she may finally get her chance.

"I really don't get it, Ava." I look up from my phone, trying to shove the wretched jealous feelings down. "I know this test is important to him, but would you be hanging out with the enemy if you were in his shoes?"

"I would never hang out with that girl for any reason. She's awful." She sits down across from me, crossing her legs. "But guys are different, Lex. When they get into fights, they punch it out and then shake hands afterwards. It's like they forget what they were even arguing about in the first place. So, I don't think they think like us when it comes to this stuff."

I shake my head. "There's no way I could forget what Sienna did."

That girl was so jealous I'd been given the lead role in the spring recital that she went straight to our dance instructor and told Ms. Halloway I'd been mean to the girls and that I didn't deserve to be principal. Then, she went and told the girls I'd been saying all these awful things about them: calling them fat, ugly, bad dancers. They all believed her lies and shunned me, giving me glares the moment I entered the studio.

I'd never once said one cruel thing about any of them, but I'd been painted as the ice bitch when really that was Sienna. She was the one who talked badly about them behind their backs. She was the one who called them fat. I honestly don't know why I was ever friends with her. Except, at that age, I think I was afraid if I wasn't nice to her that she'd be mean to me too.

After that, coming to class was no longer fun. And Ms. Halloway seemed to fall in line with her students even though she'd known me since I was a little girl and knew what kind of person I was—or should've known. She started criticizing my every move and warned me that if I didn't change my attitude, I'd lose the lead and be kicked out of the studio. So...I left.

I was done being treated like the bad guy, and it was clear no one was going to take my side. It was fifteen against one. So, Sienna finally got what she wanted. But even after she took the lead role, her bullying didn't stop. She still tries to sink her claws in, only, my friends know exactly the type of person I am —and exactly who she is. Although, after what I saw tonight, it looks like she may have finally won.

"All I can say is Jaxon would be an idiot to date her." She

shakes her head. "She's the queen of snobbery and he deserves so much better. But guys tend to think with their you-know-whats, so personality doesn't always factor in."

In other words, Sienna is pretty, and Jaxon's dick may want to get to know her better. A thought I detest more than Sienna herself. It's not that I just don't want to see Jaxon get hurt or waste his time on someone who doesn't deserve his attention, but the thought of him spending time with anyone in that way bothers me.

Again, this is exactly why I shouldn't have had sex with him yesterday. Now, I can't even think past my jealousy. This is so not good.

Ava's cell phone dings with a text and I cling to the mental distraction, watching her take out her phone and check it. Suddenly, her entire demeanor changes. Shoulders tensing. Cheeks reddening, and I'm wondering who it's from and what it says.

"What's wrong, Ava?"

She quickly taps on the screen then looks up. "Nothing. Just a spam text. I'm going to go grab us something to eat. Any requests?"

She hops up from the floor, seeming frazzled. But maybe she's just worried because she opened the thing. I'm always freaking out if I accidentally open spam, panicking that some virus has been attached and my phone will crash.

"Any kind of junk food works," I answer.

She darts from the room, leaving me all alone with my thoughts. I hop up and go in search of the TV remote to keep myself from traveling back down the road of regret and confusion again. It's not in any of the obvious places, so I try her nightstand drawer. The moment I pull it open, I nearly jump, letting out a little yelp when I see a massive dildo laying inside with a ribbon tied around it and a yellow sticky note attached that says... "A present for our little prude."

What the hell?

Ava's shy, and although she's really pretty, she keeps her nose stuck in her books. And when she's not reading, or going to some church event with Mercy, she's babysitting. So, who on earth would be giving her a *gift* like that? And why would she keep it? Although maybe I know why she'd want to keep the thing. It looks kind of fun.

The sound of footsteps coming back down the hall has me quickly shutting her drawer and moving away. I don't want her to think I'm snooping through her things, but now I'm more than curious as to what's going on with my dear friend.

"Okay," she says, walking back in. "I've got cookies, chips, and candy. And chicken parm is on its way."

"Aw, thanks, Ava."

I take the cookies and a water bottle from her, needing to shove a treat into my mouth before I ask her the question that's on the tip of my tongue. I'm dying to know who the hell got her the biggest dildo I've ever seen, but then she'll know I was in her drawer. I need to find a way to get her to open the thing in front of me. Then I can hit her with all of my questions.

"Hey, Ava?"

"Yeah?" She places everything down on the desk.

"Do you have a coaster? I don't want a water ring to form on the wood."

"Good point." She nods, rushing over to her nightstand where I saw one lying next to the big plastic cock. She opens the drawer, letting out a surprised squeak of her own, and slams it shut. "I'll have to go get one from the living room. Be right back."

Once again, she's frazzled and red in the face, but I can't ask her what's going on because she clearly doesn't want me seeing the thing. Hence, her freak-out and near slamming of her fingers. There's seriously something going on with her, and I'm going to have to ask Mercy about it. If anyone knows, she will.

The two of them are like sisters; they share the same kind of bond as Jax and I do—or as we used to. Now, it seems Jaxon's keeping secrets from me. But unfortunately for him, I walked into the wrong place at the wrong time.

CHAPTER 8

Jaxon

The second the bell rings, I'm out of my seat, rushing toward the door. I need to catch Lexie before she evades me again.

"Mr. Miller." Mrs. Jansen's voice stops me in my tracks. I turn, keeping the sigh locked behind gritted teeth. Of all the days she could hold me back, this had to be the one.

"I just wanted to let you know that you got a hundred on your paper. It was very well written, Jaxon. In fact, it was one of the best submitted in all my classes. So, I'm happy to inform you that you now have a B in my class and no longer need to worry about me having that discussion with Coach Rally. Now, I hope you keep up the good work and don't let things slip again." She gives me a pointed look. "And I hope you boys bring home that trophy."

"Thanks, Mrs. Jansen. I won't." I tip my head, smiling. "And we plan on it. Have a good weekend."

I turn and rush out the door, the relief from that good news not hitting like it should. With the way things have been between me and Lex, it feels like I sold my soul to the devil for that grade. Now, instead of being stuck on the sidelines on the field, I've been benched from Lexie's life. And with the way this feels, I'd rather have been kicked off the team.

All week she's been blowing me off, claiming she's tied up with the girls and cheer, but I'm calling bullshit. She's barely spoken to me at lunch. And I've noticed how she stopped coming to her locker in the mornings. Every day I've waited for her, but she hasn't shown. Clearly, she's pissed about my study date with Sienna. But what I don't understand is why she told me she was cool with it.

I scan the parking lot, on the lookout for her Jeep, crossing my fingers she hasn't taken off yet. She and I need to have a chat. Face to face so I can see her eyes when I ask her why she's giving me the cold shoulder. My stomach eases up when I spot my pretty girl standing by Cord's truck, chatting and laughing with all our friends. At least she didn't make a run for it, trying to dodge me again—like she's done all week.

I make my way over, drinking her in with every step. Damn, she looks gorgeous today in that tight little black bodysuit and gold and black plaid skirt. She's already getting into the spirit of Halloween and looks like a naughty little witch in those black knee-high leather boots. And man, do I want to be the broom she rides on. My Lexie Lou loves the haunted holiday probably more than she loves Christmas—and I love seeing all the sexy costumes she dresses up in.

I sneak up behind her, wrapping my arms around her waist, causing her to yelp in surprise. "Boo," I say, planting a kiss on her cheek.

"Jaxon!" she gasps, stiffening in my arms. See. This is what I'm talking about. She hates me. I can't even give her a hug without her turning to ice. Here I was hoping to change our relationship status from friends to forever, but now, I'll be lucky if she'll even smile at me again.

She shifts out of my arms, moving to stand between Mercy and Ava: her two bodyguards who've been flanking her sides all week. "Okay, so are we on for the Fright House tonight?" Lex asks the girls, once again, ignoring my existence. This is what it's been like all week. I'm not even benched on her side of the playing field anymore. It's like I'm from the opposing team.

The girls all say yes to the plan, but Piper shakes her head no.

"What? You're not coming?" Lexie's face drops. I know she was excited to go with the girls since none of them have been before. But Lex is all about inclusivity, so if one doesn't want to go, she'd rather pass and do something else so no one's left out. Another one of her sweet traits that makes me love her that much more.

"Come on, Pipe," Samantha chimes in. "It will be so much fun. Besides, it's our senior year. Next year we're going to be scattered across the country for Halloween. This may be our last chance to do this together. Please?" She gives Piper pleading puppy dog eyes. "You have to come with us."

Piper looks to be struggling with her decision. She's a little scaredy cat. Won't even watch any horror movies. She even gets scared by the witch in *Snow White*, so I know she's terrified of the idea of being in the haunted house. But I don't want my Lex to miss out on this. And she will if her friend doesn't go. She'll stay behind and hang out with Piper instead.

"Come on, Pipster," I say. "If you come, we'll promise to leave you alone."

Practically the entire football team works at the Fright House, so all we have to do is tell them to tone it down for Piper, and the girl will get the Disney Haunted Mansion version instead of the House of Horrors experience.

"You're not the one I'm worried about, Jax." Her eyes dart to Drake. "He is."

Can't say I blame her suspicions on that one. Drake is the king of mischief. He's usually the one that comes up with the most brutal pranks for Fright Night. He also happens to be the master of the scare team at the Fright House.

"Who, me?" he says, with a wicked gleam in his eyes. "Hey, I'll go easy on you, Pipsqueak. Promise." He crosses a finger over his heart, but still has the mischievous grin on his face.

All I can say is he better not try to mess with Piper tonight, because Cord will serve him his ass on a platter if he does. And if Cord doesn't, I will. Lex will feel awful if Piper doesn't have a good time tonight and ends up with nightmares afterwards.

My phone buzzes in my pocket. I pull it out, seeing I have a text from Rye McGavin, the guy who hardly speaks to anyone other than his stepbrother. So, what the heck does he want with me?

Rye: Thought you'd like to know that TJ Montgomery was talking about your girl today. Said he's planning on making a move. Probably going to ask Lex to the Fright Ball. Figured you'd like to know so you can get off your ass and stake a claim on your girl.

The fuck? How the heck does Rye know how I feel about Lexie? Not that I don't appreciate the heads-up, but he and I barely even cross paths. He's part of the baseball team and they tend to keep to themselves. Just like us football players do. It's not that we don't mingle with others; we just spend so much time with our teammates—before school, after school, weekends—that we've naturally become like a brotherhood.

Drake, Banner, and Cord are like brothers, but even they don't know how I feel about Lex. I figured if I shared with one of them, they'd all find out. And if Cord found out, he'd share with his stepsister. And Piper would share with my girl. So, I've kept my mouth shut.

Me: Thanks for the heads-up. You hear anything else, let me know.

Like hell I'm going to let Montgomery swoop in and steal Lex from me. Problem is she *isn't* mine yet. And with how mad she is, he stands a chance. Which means, I need to do something. *Now.*

"Okay, so do you girls want to come over around seven?" Lex asks. "I'll order pizza and we can just hang out until it's time to get ready. Then we'll head to the Fright House at ten. Does that work?"

Works for me. That gives me three hours to get through to her. I'm going to head to her house where she won't be able to dodge me or use the "I'm studying" excuse since it's a Friday. But…I'm not showing up empty-handed, which means I need to run a few errands.

* * *

LEXIE'S MOM opens the door, smiling as soon as she sees me. "Hey, Jax. Come on in. Girls are upstairs."

Girls? I thought they weren't coming over until seven. You've got to be kidding me. Now, I have to sit on pins and needles for another night. Fucking fabulous.

I nod, forcing a smile. "Thanks, Mrs. G."

Before I reach the top of the stairs, I dig the present out of the bag and tuck it into my pocket where it's going to be burning a hole until I can give it to her.

"Knock! Knock!" I say, entering through her open door and nearly tripping over my feet when I see Lex standing in front of her mirror, dressed in a sexy nurse's costume. My thoughts get "sick" real fast, and the throbbing ache that's now pressing at the seam of my jeans wants to be cared for.

Lex spins around, crossing her arms. Her smile turning into a straight line. Her shiny mood dulling at my arrival when once upon a time—as in last week—she would've bounced over and practically jumped into my arms, giving me the biggest hug, happy to see me.

"What are you doing here, Jax?"

The ice she's trying to freeze me out with is cold, but I'm determined to get past this. Determined to win her love back. It's like fighting past a wall of muscle to get into the end zone, but if you push hard enough, dig your feet in the ground and don't give up, you get through and score. And that's what my ultimate goal is. I don't want the trophy; I want Lexie.

"I just wanted to stop by. Brought over some candy for you girls, too." I wink, holding out the bag of goodies. She has the biggest sweet tooth on the planet, and I was hoping to sugar her up with some chocolate before we talked. But now it looks like she and Samantha will be indulging in my gesture.

Lexie doesn't budge, staring at the bag as if it's filled with poison. Sam steps forward, taking it from me and shooting me an apologetic look. She's probably gotten an earful this week on how I'm the most awful friend in the world, but at least she isn't glaring at me like the love of my life is.

My stomach knots like I've eaten a thousand pieces of candy. I can't do this anymore. We can't go on like this. I'm losing my best friend. And for what? Because I spent a few hours with Sienna so I could pass my test? No! That's bullshit. We're hashing this shit out NOW.

"Can we talk, Lex?"

"You can see that I'm busy." She glances toward Sam who's dressed as a white angel, though she looks far from angelic. The monsters at the Fright House are going to go crazy when they see her; one in particular is going have a fit when he sees how much skin she's revealing in that white satin bustier. "We'll have to talk later."

"You're always busy," I grumble, no longer able to hide my frustration. She's been busy all week, doing a standup job of keeping me out of her life when we almost never went a day without hanging out, or at least talking on the phone for hours. "You ever going to make time for me again?"

"My social calendar is kind of full." She cocks her stubborn chin up. "But maybe Sienna is free."

Fucking hell. She's throwing this shit back in my face. I glance over at Sam, ready to ask her for some privacy, but she shakes her head at me as if warning me that now is not the time. I beg to differ since I'm losing my mind. But then again, Lex will be even more pissed at me if I do this now, while her friend is over. Then she won't hear a word I have to say. Her stubborn ears will be closed off. And I'll be digging myself a bigger hole, which I sure as hell don't want to do.

"I'll see you ladies at the Fright House tonight."

I turn and stalk from her room, my feet feeling like lead weights as I descend the stairs. This is not how I saw this going. I was going to smooth talk my way in, sugar her up with sweets and heartfelt apologies, then show her exactly how I feel about her.

"You're heading out already, Jax?" Mrs. Grayson asks, coming out of the kitchen.

More like being kicked out. "Yep." I nod. "Don't want to intrude on girl time."

"Okay. Well, we'll see y'all on Sunday."

"See you then."

At least I know Lex will be forced to spend time with me then. Our parents have made it a rule that family dinner nights are sacred, and no one can back out or make other plans, so it looks like she won't be able to avoid me forever.

CHAPTER 9

Lexie

This place is scarier than I expected it to be, but I need to stay strong for Piper. I don't want her regretting her decision to come with us tonight. But as the doors open for us to enter the main part of the Fright House, for our journey into terror to begin, I'm already afraid. The special effects in this place are incredible. They make everything seem so real. We've only been through the front corridor where they welcomed us with a horrifying warning and I'm already freaking out.

I step into the next room, trying to remain calm, appear amused. Drake mentioned how the monsters feed on people who look scared and jumpy, and I definitely don't want that to be me. The fog billows around us like a thick cloud, barely allowing me to see past a foot in front of me. Eerie sounds are coming from every direction; distant screams from other victims touring the house ahead of us, showing me exactly what I have to look forward to. Awesome.

We keep walking forward, slowly. I'm waiting for someone to jump out at us, but as far as I can tell, there's nothing in this room. It's completely empty, not even filled with spooky props. But then…the fog clears, and a wall of doors appears. Each one is guarded by a monster. And there's no getting out of this room until we approach one. Yikes!

There's a tap on my shoulder and I nearly jump. "Go to that one," Piper says, pointing to the one with a creepy clown in front of it.

I nod, trying to gulp down my dread and some air at the same time. I no longer want to be the leader in front of the girl pack. But if I show fear, Piper will lose her shit, so I step forward, reminding myself that it's all fake. It's all an act. Just makeup and really freaking good special effects. But as I get closer to the clown, I feel like I'm the kid in the Stephen King movie, walking into the hands of my murderer. About to be pulled into the drain and slaughtered.

"Are you sure you want to come this way, girls?" the clown asks, and my nerves take a nosedive into my stomach. I'd recognize his voice in my sleep. In fact, it's been haunting my dreams all week. "They won't play nice if you enter this door. At least, not with you, Lex."

I grit my teeth and cross my arms. "Had I known it was you, I would have chosen another door. Now move, Jax."

At least with all the creepy makeup he has on, it's easier to be mad at him. Maybe he should wear this costume permanently and then I won't struggle so much with my attraction. I'm not even sure what I'm more upset with anymore—what he did, or how my body won't respond to anything other than thoughts of him and his incredible dick.

Every time I think of him, I get horny. Every time I see him, I get butterflies. When I hear his voice, a shiver runs through my shoulders. And every time I've tried to masturbate this week, I've only been able to reach my peak if I picture his thick cock and how demanding it was. Not to mention the hot and heavy dreams that have been waking me up in a sweat with an ache between my legs that's almost unbearable.

Jax lets out a growl fit for a monster, though I don't think he's in character right now. I think he's frustrated that I'm not smiling and acting like he's the center of my world anymore. But why would I? He hasn't even apologized for what he did. Not one single "sorry" has come from his mouth.

"Fine," he grits through his teeth. "But don't say I didn't warn you, Lex."

I shove past him, turning the knob and charging into the next room, not paying a lick of attention to anything other than my frazzled thoughts. Until...I run right into another clown.

His hands reach out to steady me, lingering a little too long for my liking. He lets out an evil chuckle and I swear I'm on the *It* movie set.

"You should watch where you're going," he says, his voice as evil-sounding as his costume. "Now, you're mine, little nurse." His eyes scan down my body, landing on my chest and making my skin crawl with the creepies. "I think I feel sick. Will you take care of me?" He closes in on my personal space, and with each step back I take, he stalks forward.

"No. She's going to take care of me," sneers another clown who suddenly appears by my side, his face too close to mine. His hot breath on my cheek. Predatory eyes mentally stripping me under his stare.

I shift to the right, trying to move away from them, but they follow in pursuit, leaving me no room to breathe. I know their job is to scare people, but this doesn't feel right. Their lecherous stares are all too real, and I don't think hitting on girls is part of their job description. I'm pretty sure this place would be shut down if that was happening.

"How about we share?" the one on the left says.

"I like that idea." The other one grins, his red smile going from ear to ear, showing off the red makeup that's now smeared all over his teeth. "She can take care of both of us. What do you say, little one? Do you think you can handle two clowns at once? Bandaging his BIG booboo while you lick my very sore wound?"

My body trembles. I'm seriously regretting my choice in costume. And regretting suggesting we come here in the first place. I thought this was supposed to be fun. But I am not having fun. I'm about to have a panic attack.

"She's mine, fuckers. Back away now." Jaxon's dominant voice booms through the room, sending a shiver down my spine. God, I'm so glad he's here.

"We didn't realize she'd already been claimed. Sorry, man," the one on the left says as they both back away, finally giving me space to breathe, although I'm still not doing a lot of that. Both hold their hands up, no longer sounding as terrifying as they had a moment ago. I wonder if they're scared of Jaxon. They should be. He's bigger than both of them. "We'll just have to find ourselves another nurse to make us feel all better."

They continue their retreat, then turn and rush through another door while I nearly slump on Jaxon. "Thank you" is on the tip of my tongue, but before I get the words out, he grips onto my arm and starts leading me toward the back corner of the room, taking me away from the girls.

"What are you doing, Jax?" I try pulling away, but he refuses to let me go, his grip getting tighter. Just having his touch on me is too much for my senses. I'm too on edge in this place. I can't also deal with my body's emotions right now.

"You're coming with me," he growls in the same tone he had with the two creepers, kicking my frustration up to a ten.

"No, I'm not, Jax." I stop in place, stomping my heel down. "I'm not going anywhere with you, you jerk."

"You don't have a choice." He leans in close. Too close for what I can handle right now. His teeth are gritted, and his eyes have never been so intense. "I warned you not to enter this room, Lex, but you didn't listen. Too fucking bad. Now, you're mine."

That word sends a blast of tingles shooting through my veins, causing me to lose my focus long enough for him to bend down and throw me over his shoulder. He hauls me through a door and into a dark hallway, leaving the girls behind in the other room. I pound on his back, demanding he put me down, but he doesn't. Not until we're in what looks to be the Fright House storage room. Where freaky mechanical dolls line the walls, and coffins and spooky props fill most of the space.

"Jax, take me back to the girls," I huff, shifting my dress back down so my butt isn't showing. I whip my blonde curls out of my face and straighten my hat back into place, wishing I could straighten out my emotions too.

"No." He crosses his arms, widening his stance and blocking the doorway with his huge, rigid frame. The crazy clown costume only making him look more menacing. "Not until we talk."

"There's nothing we need to talk about." I cross *my* arms and lock my jaw, too. I can be just as stubborn, so he shouldn't test me.

"Really?" He cocks his red-painted chin. "Then why don't you explain why you've been avoiding me all week? And why you threw shade at me in front of Sam? I thought you understood why I was with Sienna. You texted how nice it was of her to help me."

The fact that I actually have to spell it out for him is pissing me off. He should know exactly why I'm hurt. Not only did he lie and turn to my nemesis for help, but all week Sienna's been rubbing it in my face. Giving me an evil smirk anytime she sees me. I even heard her bragging to her friends about Jaxon being so sweet on their "date" and paying for dinner. She clearly had the impression it meant more to him than what he's claiming. And even if that's not the case, he should never have put me in this position. He empowered her. He showed her that my feelings don't matter. He gave her respect when she doesn't even deserve an ounce of it. Because it clearly only enabled her further.

"Of course, I said that." I huff. "I didn't want you to fail your test. But you're supposed to have my back. Out of everyone, you're supposed to be on my team. But you turned to my bully for help. You went offsides, Jaxon. And now, she thinks she's won."

"She hasn't won shit." He shakes his head. "God, Lex. Who the fuck cares what Sienna thinks? It doesn't matter. And it shouldn't. Let the bitch think whatever she wants. We know the truth and that's all that counts."

"I care!" I shout. I can't believe he would say that. He hasn't lived in my shoes. He has no idea how it feels. She took my dream away and has done everything she can to make my life miserable ever since. It matters to me, and therefore, it should matter to him. But clearly it doesn't. Apparently, he thinks I should just move on with my life and act like everything the witch has done is completely fine. That it's all in the past.

"Take me back to the girls, Jax." I'm ready to be back with my *loyal* friends. The ones who wouldn't cozy up with my bully just to pass a test. The ones who would stare the girl down and tell her to fuck off no matter what she was offering. If he truly cared about me and my feelings, his dick wouldn't even look in her direction.

"No!" He steps closer, towering over me, his loud booming voice shuddering through my shoulders. "We're not leaving this room until we talk about this. This is ridiculous, Lex. You're the one letting her win. Not me."

Ridiculous? He thinks I'm being ridiculous? I step up onto my tippy toes, getting right in his stupid clown face. "No, Jax. There's nothing left for us to say. And you know what's ridiculous? The fact that your grade was more important than your best friend's feelings. Now take me back to the girls."

"Fine," he grits through his teeth. "If your stubborn ass is going to act like a brat then I guess we're done here."

Brat? Really? Wow, that's rich coming from the guy who's acting like a complete barbaric asshole.

I go to push past him, ready to be out of this place, but he blocks me again. He crouches down then suddenly I'm over his shoulder again and he's leading me back down the dark hallway where eerie screams echo in the distance. But they're not as loud as the ones going off in my head. In all the times we have ever fought, I've never been so mad. Or so hurt. The pain is slicing right through.

I don't understand why he can't see it from my side. It's like he doesn't even care how I feel. And that's what drives the knife in deeper. I thought he'd be fighting for me right now. That he'd be apologizing for not thinking about how it would make me feel. I wanted him to beg me to forgive him. But instead, he's calling me a brat and dismissing my feelings.

"What's it gonna take for you to forgive me, Lex?"

Maybe an apology would help, asshole. Realizing what he did wrong would be a good start. But he hasn't done either of those things. He's told me I'm being ridiculous. Called me a stubborn brat.

"If you think I'm going to forgive you now, you're wrong."

He turns, taking us down another dark hallway. It feels like I'm in some kind of old dungeon with stone walls and flickering candles everywhere.

"You keep stabbing me with that threat, Lex, but you won't even listen to my side."

His side? He had the chance to talk and all he did was tell me I'm stupid for hating Sienna. Apparently, he thinks I should be perfectly fine with the fact that the girl now believes she has the one-up on me because my best friend took her to dinner and flirted with her.

"Your side? You've clearly turned to the dark side. And that's all I need to know." He turns another corner, winding us deeper into this place. "Jaxon let me go! If you think I'm going to talk you now, you're wrong!"

"You refuse to talk to me anyway. Can't get your stubborn ass to listen to a damn thing."

And there he goes again calling me names. There's one name I would like to call him: LIAR. "Why should I listen to you when all you tell me are lies?"

He suddenly stops walking but doesn't put me down. A loud clanking sound starts behind us, sounding like a heavy metal door opening. "Trouble in paradise?" says another voice I recognize—Drake's here. Awesome. Now, we're going to have the whole damn football team witnessing our fight. Just what I need: drama. Jax should know that after what happened with Sienna, I hate drama.

Jaxon ignores his comment, carrying me forward again and then stops and finally places me back on my feet. The blood rushes back down from my head and my vision spins along with my emotions. He steps forward, pointing me with a look that sends my nerves up in flames.

"You can say what you want, babe. Scream and punch me for all I care, but I'm not letting you go."

I cross my arms, trying to close myself off from the pain. Even when Sienna tore my love of dance away, turned my world upside down, it didn't hurt as much as this. "You let me go the moment you went out with Sienna," I say, trying to keep the tears at bay. The last thing I want to do is crumble. Especially not in front of our friends.

Jaxon stares at me, the strained silence ticking on while my mind yells for him to fight for me. I want him to make the pain go away. To fix us before it's too late. But he just stands there and says nothing. Does nothing.

"Come on, Jax," Drake says. "We have a job to do."

Jaxon stares for one more beat, an angry clown glaring at his wounded victim. Then he turns his back on me and exits the cell, locking me inside with Sam and Ava.

My heart splinters down the center. I'm losing my best friend. And God, it hurts. Probably more so because I slept with him. And now...I'm positive I'm in love with him. But it's more than obvious nothing is ever going to happen between us. He doesn't even care enough about me to apologize.

CHAPTER 10

Lexie

The moment the girls leave and the silence hits, the noise inside my head nearly deafens me. I wish my parents were here to distract me, but they're gone for the day and won't be back until tomorrow morning. Which means I'm alone with my brutal thoughts.

"Alexa, please play my cleaning playlist."

"Okay," her robotic voice answers. "Playing cleaning playlist."

Music starts filling the space but not loud enough to stop my mind from replaying everything that happened last night. Recalling everything Jaxon said and did. Mainly what he didn't say and didn't do.

"Alexa, please turn up the volume."

"Turning up volume."

The only way to stop thinking is to keep myself busy, so I start in the living room, cleaning up all our candy wrappers and dishes from last night. Throwing all the blankets into the wash. I load the dishwasher. Then wipe down the counters. Going extra for my mom and cleaning out the fridge too. Clearing out any expired food and rotting produce. Then I grab the vacuum and run it around the kitchen, making my way back into the living room. I make sure to run it under the couch where I know I dropped a Raisinet last night.

The vacuum suddenly makes a strange noise like it's swallowed up a curtain. I pull it out from under the couch and shut it off, finding a yellow sticky note stuck in the roller. I tug it free, seeing the words written in black ink and perfect penmanship. The same handwriting as the sticky note I saw inside Ava's drawer.

It's only a matter of time, Ava.

What the heck? Time for what? And why is my dear friend getting these weird notes? Does she have a secret admirer she's not telling us about? More like a stalker based on the creep factor going on. First the giant dildo, and then this.

But if that were the case, why wouldn't she mention it? She hasn't said a word about anything. Hasn't even hinted to something weird going on. Nothing. Nada. Zilch. But something is definitely going on with our friend.

I think it's time to give her a call and get to the bottom of this. At least now I have a reason to ask her point blank.

"Alexa, please turn off the music."

The music stops and I dial Ava's number. Five rings and it goes to voicemail.

"Hey, Ava. It's Lex. Need to talk to you about something. Give me a call when you have a chance. Love ya."

As soon as I end the call, it immediately starts ringing in my hand. But it's not Ava returning my call, it's Jaxon. I reject the call, sending him to voicemail, like I've done all the other times he called last night. This time, he doesn't leave a message. But then my phone dings with an incoming text.

Jaxon: Lex, please talk to me. I'm really sorry about last night. It was just supposed to be a stupid prank.

A stupid prank? They locked us in the dungeon, then terrorized us in the dark. I begged him to let us out, but he didn't budge. Once again, proving where his loyalty lies—not with me. If he cared so much about me and our fragile friendship, he would've let us out of the cell and told his football buddies to fuck off. But he didn't.

I open the text, making sure he knows it's been read, but I'm not responding. He has yet to apologize for what really matters. And until he does, I don't have anything to say to him.

The frustration boils up. I think it's time to go for a run. I grab my earbuds and sneakers and head out the door, only to realize three minutes in what a bad idea it was. Now, I'm even more alone with my thoughts. Each stride pounding in another horrible truth. I'm not running off my frustration; it feels like I'm running towards it. Unable to take any more, I flip around and run right back to my house.

"Alexa, please blast my pump-it-up playlist." I head straight up to my bathroom, hoping to wash away some of this mental grime. But unfortunately, no amount of scrubbing or shaving takes the pain away either. As soon as I get dried and dressed, I go in search of my phone. It's time to call the girls. If I keep this bottled up anymore, I'm going to explode.

When my screen unlocks, it shows I have twelve missed texts. But not a single one is from Jaxon. They're all from the "Fearsome Five."

Samantha: Okay, so we need to iron out the details on how to steal the trophy. We also need to decide on what we want our ransom to be. Do we want them to pay cash that we'll donate somewhere? Or be our personal slaves? Thoughts?

Clearly, Sam has one thing on the brain: revenge for what the guys did last night. But based on the argument she had with Drake, I think there's another motive for her revenge. I think something may have happened between the two enemies that she's not sharing. It seems like all of my friends are keeping secrets.

Mercy: I've been thinking about it, Sam. And I don't really like the plan. What if we get caught on camera? We'll be suspended.

That's a good point. None of us want to jeopardize our school records right now. Especially not when colleges are trying to decide if we're a good fit or not. I definitely don't want to risk my chance with Michigan.

Ava: She's right. We need to come up with something else. Besides, I don't want to punish the whole football team, just the four who locked us in that cell.

Samantha: I guess you're right. Okay, so let's do something off school grounds. Oh wait. How about this. While the guys are working that night, we'll have their trucks towed to the scrap yard. They'll have to make a public apology and grovel in order to find out where their trucks are.

Man, she's evil. I'm all about getting the guys back, but that's a bit much.

Mercy: No. I think that's too extreme. Banner's an asshole, but I don't want to damage their personal property. What if the trucks get messed up? Or get scrapped before the guys get to them?

Have to say, I never thought I'd see the day when Mercy was calling Banner an asshole. She's been in love with that boy since kindergarten. The big dreamy-eyed follow-him-around kind of love. But after what he did to her last night, I don't blame her. Banner's another one on my shit list right now.

Samantha: Fine, Miss Goody-Two-shoes. We won't mess with their trucks.

Ava: Is there anything other than football and girls that the guys care about?

Samantha: Their big-ass egos. LOL

Samantha: Earth to Lex and Piper? Do you two have any ideas?

Samantha: Guess they're busy. But I just thought of something. What if we dare the guys to meet us at the old, abandoned Winthrop house. Then we'll lock them inside and give them their own frightening experience. Maybe we can even get some of the basketball players to help out.

Now, that's a good idea. Give them a taste of their own medicine.

Mercy: Oh, I like that plan. That place gives me the creeps.

Ava: I think that's perfect. They locked us in the dark cell, so we'll lock them in that creepy house and see how they like it.

I'm definitely on board with the plan and know exactly who to ask for help.

Me: Sorry, I was in the shower. Yes. Sounds like a good plan. I'll ask TJ if the guys would be willing to be our own personal scare team.

I'm sure he'll agree. TJ's one of the nicest guys. Plus, I'm pretty sure he has a thing for me. One of the girls on the cheer team said she heard he was going to ask me to the Fright Ball. I wish the idea gave me warm fuzzies, but it doesn't. There's only one person who I want as my date, but we aren't even speaking right now. And even if we do ever get past this fight, I'm not even sure he'll ask me.

Samantha: We'll wait to see what Piper thinks, but I think it's the perfect revenge. And while the boys are locked inside that house getting the shit scared out of them, I'll fill the bed of Drake's truck with trash and see how he likes it.

I roll my eyes. Sam is always poking the bear. It's crazy to think she and Drake used to be best friends. Now, their hatred for each other knows no bounds.

"Knock! Knock!"

My heart leaps into my throat as I nearly jump off the bed.

"Jaxon! What are you doing in here? You scared the crap out of me." I press my hand over my chest, trying to calm my racing heart—but just seeing him causes it to beat faster.

"I knocked and rang the doorbell, but you must not have

heard over the music. We need to talk, Lex. I'm done with you ignoring my calls."

The nerves grip my stomach, the tension descending in my room like smog. I'm ready to tell Jax to fuck off, but I bite back the words as I take in the sight of him. He looks like a mess. In fact, I've never seen Jaxon looking so out of sorts. There's a heaviness hanging over him, a sadness in his eyes. He's also sporting a shadow of scruff like he hasn't shaved in days, and his sexy shaggy hair looks like his fingers waged a war with it.

"Lex, I'm sorry." He steps forward. Cautiously. As if he's afraid I'll spook. "I'm not just sorry about last night. I'm sorry that I hurt you."

He sits down next to me on the bed, taking my hand in his and locking our fingers together. A warmth runs up my arm and settles right in the left side of my chest.

"It's the last thing I meant to do. I was just so worried about my grade that I didn't think past my own situation. I didn't think about how it'd make you feel or what kind of message it would send to Sienna." He hangs his head, letting out a pained sigh. "God, babe, if I could go back in time, I'd tell Sienna to fuck off. I never should've made you feel like I wasn't in your corner. That I didn't have your back."

He looks up, eyes meeting mine, sincerity burning in their depths. "I'd rather be kicked off the team than lose you, Lex. You mean so damn much to me, babe."

My vision blurs with unshed tears, and the pain that's been trapped inside my thoughts slips away like a leaf on a stream. This is what I've been longing to hear. What I needed to be whole again.

I shift forward, climbing up onto his lap and wrap my arms around his shoulders. Sinking into the warmth of his tight embrace and snuggling into his neck.

"Tell me you forgive me, baby."

I nod, the emotions closing up my throat as the tears finally slip down my cheeks. "I forgive you, Jax." How could I not? We've been through so much together. And he's right, Sienna is not worth losing our friendship over.

He hugs me even closer, tucking me into his big burly nook. "God, I've missed you, Lexie Lou."

"I've missed you, too." I breathe past the emotion. "I never want to fight again."

"Me neither." He kisses the top of my head. "This week's been hell."

Guilt creeps in, knowing that I intentionally iced him out. He's not the only one who needs to apologize.

"Jax." I sit back and wipe my eyes. "I'm sorry that I didn't think past my hatred for Sienna and understand where you were coming from. I'm glad you passed the test, regardless of how it happened. It was important and I shouldn't have made you feel guilty over it. And you were right." I lean forward and press a kiss on the end of his nose. "Her opinion doesn't matter. And shouldn't matter. It's us and our incredible friendship that matters."

His adorable grin has my cheeks warming with a flush of heat.

"You're definitely forgiven, Lex, but under one condition."

"What's that?" My brow raises.

"You'll go to the Fright Ball with me?"

Now I'm the one grinning big. "Of course, I'll be your date. I wouldn't want to go with anyone else." I squeeze him again, planting another kiss on his cheek. When I shift back, I feel something hard beneath my butt. Immediately realizing what's pressing against me.

My body heats. My mind starts spinning with confusion again. His reaction could simply be due to the friction it's been getting as I shift around on his lap. Or...it could be because he's remembering our moment together. Our mistake. Which we can *never* make again. Our friendship means too much to me, and I won't do anything to risk losing it again. This last week was too painful.

Before temptation takes me under its control, I need to get off of his lap, and we need to get out of this bed.

"Hey!" I say, scooting off him and standing. "Do you want to go to the Halloween store with me so we can pick out costumes for the dance? Plus, we still haven't gotten things for the Fright Bash yet, and the party's coming up in two weeks."

He gives me a look that I'm struggling to decipher, but finally his cheeks tip up with a smile. "Sure." He nods. "I owe you a date. So how about we have a redo. Halloween store, dinner, and a movie?"

I nod excitedly. Public spaces are good. Being surrounded by lots of people will definitely help distract my thoughts. "We could see *Deviant Behavior*?" I suggest.

"I thought you saw it already."

"No." The memory of that night sneaks back in, and jealousy wants to rear its ugly head again. "Wasn't really feeling up to the movies that night."

His smile drops again and guilt falls like a shadow on his face. He reaches for me, pulling me between his legs and taking my cheek in his hand. "I'm truly sorry, babe."

"I know you are." I nod, nuzzling into his palm. "We're good, Jax. It's water under the bridge. Promise." I kiss his palm then smile. "And I promise not to be a typical girl and throw it in your face any time we argue in the future."

He chuckles, shaking his head. "You've never been a typical girl, Lex. You've always been a wonder. Sometimes stubborn"— he winks—"but always perfect."

Butterflies flip in my stomach. Those totally inappropriate feelings rushing back in. And when his eyes land on my lips, looking as if he wants to kiss me, my heart does a somersault, praying that he takes the plunge and crosses the forbidden line.

But then…he pulls away and stands. "All right, you ready to head out so we have time to pack it all in?"

I know this is for the best, but I can't help the disappointment I feel. "Yep, let me just change out of these sweats and I'll be ready."

I go into my closet. This time closing the door behind me. I need a minute to get my emotions under control. To breathe through this irrational sadness. It's not going to serve our friendship any good if I can't get past these feelings. Which means, I need to figure out how to convince myself that we're better off as friends. I need a friendship reboot. So that will be my goal today.

CHAPTER 11

Jaxon

"What do you think about this?" she asks, coming out of the dressing room dressed like a fucking sex goddess. She chose a genie costume: silver, shimmery, and so fucking skimpy. The little halter top is like a bra, shelving her incredible tits perfectly. And the skirt—I refrain from biting down on my fist—has slits up both sides, revealing her long, silky, tan legs. Legs I dream about having wrapped around my face. Fuck me. How the hell am I going to keep my hands to myself when she's wearing that?

"Definitely." I swallow back all the dirty things that want to slip past my watering mouth. "But I'm going to have to go with the Viking War Lord costume now to keep all the little shits from trying to cop a feel." Guys are going to be falling to their knees, begging her to make all their sexual wishes come true.

She turns around to look in the mirror again, and I get the best view of her back: her sleek, toned muscles that have been carved from years of dance and cheer. The perfect curve of her spine that I'm dying to run my lips along. Then there's the perky little rump that sits at the base, hugged by the shimmering skirt. That ass keeps my dick up at night in sweats. Like he is right now.

"I'm going to go grab my costume," I say, quickly turning and exiting the dressing room before she sees the protrusion in my pants. The last thing I want to do is mess this up. We're finally back on good terms. She's giving me her beautiful smile again, the one I wait by her locker for every morning. It's like my coffee. It fuels my veins for the day. Perks me up and pumps me full of energy. And I don't want to lose it again. Last week was the most miserable of my life.

If I cross the line with her and she's not on the same page, I'm afraid I'll be kicked to the curb. For good. And that would hurt worse than the blue balls I've been suffering from all week. That would crush me.

But then...I think of the look she had in her eyes when I almost slipped and kissed her and it has me wondering whether she wanted it. But that hope fumbles to the ground when I think of how she darted into her closet and closed the door so I couldn't see her change. She's changed in front of me our entire lives and suddenly she doesn't want me seeing her body. And I'm guessing that's because of what happened last time.

Which means, once again, I'm stuck in the damn friend zone.

"Did you find something, Jax?"

Her sweet voice pulls me from the spinning drain of my thoughts. I shake my head. Hadn't even searched for anything. "Not yet." I look along the wall at the hanging costumes and then see a Viking War Lord costume. *Bingo.* That's exactly what I'm getting. I grab an extra-large and show it to her.

"Yes." She bobs her head. "God, that's gonna look so hot on you." Her hand comes up over her mouth and her cheeks turn a feverish pink. I don't think she meant to say that out loud, but I don't understand why she's being shy. I *want* to look hot for her. She's the only one I care about what I look like for.

Until I finally woke up and realized I had feelings for her, I never noticed how I always picked clothes that I knew Lex would like. Or how I wear my ball caps backwards because I know she thinks it's sexy. All these years I've been unconsciously wanting to impress her. And now, more than ever, I want her to look at me with lust in her eyes. I want them to burn with a yearning as deep as the one in my gut.

"Okay, costumes are picked. Now, we need to go look at the animated dolls," she says, before quickly turning and darting away.

Damn, girls are confusing. I feel like I'm on a roller coaster ride. Not sure how to read her. Up. Down. Into me. Not into me. But maybe it's time to kick up the heat a notch, flirt with her a little and see how she reacts. If it seems like she's getting uncomfortable, I'll back off—spray her with silly string and play it off as a joke. But if she bites, then I'm going in for the kill.

We scan through the animated dolls, but I'm not seeing anything that's a must have. Besides, there are so many retired dolls in the Fright House storeroom that I think I'm set.

"I think we're good on dolls, Lex. You know that room I took you into last night?" Her smile drops. "We can use anything in that room. There was enough in there to fill my entire house with."

"You know, mister?" She crosses her arms, pointing her cute little nose at me. "That's another thing we need to talk about." Shit. I don't like the sound of her tone. "I'm all for the silly mischief and the stupid pranks you guys play on us each year for Fright Night. But last night was not cool. We were all scared. And look what happened to Mercy." Guilt hits her eyes and her shoulders slump. "It went too far, Jaxon."

"Yeah, I know." I shake my head, thinking of poor sweet Mercy. Banner was a dick for the stunt he pulled, but he knows it, and I think he's kicking his own ass more than we ever could.

"What Banner did wasn't part of the plan," I iterate, making sure she knows we had nothing to do with that. "I promise. Besides, we all reamed his ass out about it at practice this morning. And Cord made him run extra stadiums."

Cord should've run the damn stadiums himself, considering last night was his grand idea. He wanted to get Piper alone, so he roped us all in on his plan—wanting us to snatch up the girls then keep them occupied. But his plan backfired in his face, and now Piper's pissed at him. Serves him right.

"And as for scaring you," I continue, "we were just doing our job, Lex. You girls were in a haunted house, after all. Our job is to give you a frightening experience. But I'm sorry for scaring you. And from now on, I promise I'll only play on your team."

Her brow narrows, but I can see the amusement in the smirk she's trying to keep locked down. "Yeah, well, you better not pull something like that again. Or else…"

Her warning hangs in the air and a big question mark pops up between my legs. "Or else what?" I ask, stepping closer. "What are you going to do, Lex?"

She swallows hard, suddenly looking nervous. Her cheeks an even deeper shade of rose.

"Or else…you'll be on my shit list."

I smirk. Although, I never want to land myself a spot on her shit list again. I've never been so miserable. And the next time the guys try to rope me into one of their plans, I'm choosing my girl. They say bros before hoes. But this girl comes before all.

"Well, then, I'll make sure I behave." I step forward, removing the final gap between us. "I meant what I said, Lex. I promise to always have your back from here on out."

She leans up and presses a kiss on my cheek. The simple touch sends a jolt of tingles down my spine. I'm about to grab her chin and steal one from her lips, but then she wraps her arms around me, snuggling in for a hug. Now is clearly not the time to let my dick do my thinking. We just got through a huge fight and she needs her friend right now, not sex. But my dick happens to disagree. He thinks make-up sex is exactly what she needs.

"I will always have your back, too." She gives me one last squeeze then pulls from my hold. "Okay, I need to pick out a few more things and then we can go to dinner."

She's running off again, gathering the rest of her costume pieces while I go in search of some decorations for the party. With the way things played out last week, I didn't even think about the party. Now, I only have two weeks to get my shit together and make it the most epic one yet. Which means I need to get my head out of the heart-shaped cloud it's stuck in and get to work.

Once we're finished up at the Halloween store, we head to Tucci's, discussing the plans for the Fright Bash over dinner. Lex has already gotten almost a hundred percent of the RSVPs back and almost the entire senior class is coming, which is awesome. Also means, I'm going to need to go bigger than I ever have before. And I'm thinking a live band just may be in store. But I'm going to keep that my little secret and surprise my girl. There's a local band she's obsessed with that I'm hoping will be available for the gig.

"I'm so full," she says, sitting back and rubbing her belly. The girl can eat me under the table, yet it never shows. Probably on account of the hours she trains every day. She really is talented, always coming up with new cheers and dances. Always keeping everything fresh and making the pep rallies and half-time shows exciting. I find myself turning and watching her instead of the game whenever I'm waiting on the sidelines.

But I have to say, I wish she still danced. Lexie was like an angel up on the stage. Her body moved flawlessly and the entire audience would be mesmerized. But Sienna killed it for her. Lex was so scarred from what happened, she didn't even want to find a different dance studio. She just wanted to be out of the dance world entirely, which is a damn shame.

Man, I wish like hell I'd never even spoken to Sienna. Never will again, that's for sure. It was actually something Banner said while we were running stadiums this morning that made it click. I told him what Lex said to me last night. How me going out with her gave Sienna power, which I didn't fucking understand. That girl doesn't hold the power over anyone or anything. Hell, most of her friends don't even like her because she talks about them behind their backs. And I sure as hell don't care what that girl thinks because she's delusional.

I didn't see it until he said I sided with the enemy. And that's when I understood. By hanging out with Sienna, even if my only motive was to pass my test, it was as if I was saying that what she did to Lex didn't matter, and it sure as hell did. I never meant to give that impression, and I'll never make that mistake again.

"Earth to Jaxon!" Lex's sweet voice brings me back into focus. "Where'd you go inside that head of yours?"

"Just thinking how men really are from Venus and women are from Mars."

She bursts out laughing and I fail to see what's so funny in what I just said. It's a legit problem. Us guys don't think like they do. That's exactly what got me into the doghouse in the first place. It took an entire week of her cold shoulder for me to even decipher there was something wrong, especially when her text made it seem like everything was okay. But now I know to always read between the lines, and always make sure I'm looking straight into her eyes when I'm talking to her about anything important. Because she sure as hell can't hide her emotions from me.

"It's women are from Venus." She snorts through her laugh. "And men are from Mars."

"Whatever." I roll my eyes. "All the same to me. Y'all are aliens. That's all I need to know," I tease. She lets out a playful gasp then reaches across the table and flicks the tip of my nose.

"We are not aliens," she huffs. "Now take it back." She crosses her arms, trying to feign her offense, but she's got my favorite smile in the world splitting her cheeks.

I shake my head. "Can't take back the truth. Actually, based on recent findings, they think we're all aliens."

She scoffs at that, thinking my obsession with all the UFO documentaries is strange, but I find it fascinating. And it's educational, which I can't say the same about all the reality dating shows she loves to watch. Although, with the way I'm handling my feelings for her and caught in this awkward limbo of what the fuck I should do, maybe I should watch the dating shows. Maybe then I'd know how and when I should tell her how I feel.

"Can I get you two anything else?" Mrs. Tucci asks, coming up to the table and refilling our water glasses.

I look toward Lex who shakes her head. "No thanks, Mrs. T. We're good."

The kind woman smiles. "Okay, well, here's the check." She places it down on the table then turns to me. "And you tell that team of yours that we're counting on a win. You bring home that trophy and it will be free meatballs for everyone."

I chuckle at the gritty Italian woman who's as spicy as the sauce she whips up. "I'll let them know."

She smiles then walks away, and I reach for the bill.

"How much do I owe?" Lex asks.

I shake my head, pulling out my card. "It's on me, babe."

She gives me a look like she's confused, and it has me wishing I knew how to read minds. "Well, thanks," she finally says. "I'll get the movie tickets."

"Nope." I place my card down. "I'm getting the movie. And whatever candy treats you want, too. This date is on me, Lexie Lou."

"You don't have to do that." She shakes her head. "You don't owe me, Jax." The wind is taken right out of my sail. She's not even picking up on what I'm throwing out. I want this to be a date. A real one. Not just a "friend date."

Fuck. Maybe I should just come right out and say it. Tell her how I feel once and for all so she knows what I want. But then doubt comes barreling through and tackling that thought, leaving me second-guessing myself again. What if she doesn't feel the same? What if she shoots me down? Then what happens to our friendship? The very last thing I want to do is make things awkward between us again.

"We should probably head out if we're going to make the movie," she says, standing from the table. "I'm just going to run to the bathroom really quick."

I table my inner struggle, and nod. "Okay, I'll take care of the check and meet you up front."

She darts off to the back and I grab the bill and wave down Mrs. T, checking my phone while she goes to run my card. There's an unread message from Banner.

Banner: Dude, I need your help. Mindy is a fucking nightmare.

That's exactly what I told him when he said he was going to ask the girl out. But he didn't listen. He heard she gave the best blow jobs at our school and he went straight in for the kill. Literally, because that girl's venom is as toxic as a rattlesnake.

Me: Next time you should take your friend's advice.

Banner: Yeah, not helping. Call me in two minutes and tell me you need to meet. I'll have you on speakerphone, so make it sound believable. Like it's really important.

Me: Why can't you just tell her you're not feeling well? Make up something. Or better yet, why don't you just tell her that you're not interested???

He should cut ties now and run before he gets in any deeper with that crazy girl.

Banner: Because she sucked me off. Obviously feeling well enough to have her blow me so she's never going to buy that bullshit. BTW, the rumors are fucking false. I've had much better.

Damn, I seriously can't believe he went there. No wonder he needs a bail out.

Me: Fine, I'll bail your sorry ass out of this mess. But you need to put that dick of yours under lock and key. Then throw away the fucking key!!!

I swear. From what he did last night with Mercy, then tonight, you'd never know Banner is one of the most decent guys at our school. He seriously needs to get his shit together when it comes to girls, because these shallow relationships he keeps getting involved in aren't doing him a lick of good.

CHAPTER 12

Lexie

"Hey!" Jax says, as I come walking up to the front. He holds the door open for me and I step out into the cool night air. "Banner just texted. He needs me to call him and get him out of his date with Mindy. You have any suggestions on what I should say? You think car troubles is a good enough excuse? Or do you think Mindy will insist on coming with him to help me?"

My blood pressure immediately jumps and my happy little mood plummets. After what Banner did to Mercy last night, he deserves to be castrated. And yet, here he is, up to the same ol' shit. Using girls for sex and then drop-kicking them like a football. And even more angering is the fact that Jaxon is encouraging this shitty behavior and playing his wingman.

"No." I shake my head. "If Banner's not into her then he just needs to say that. He shouldn't string her along. It's not fair to the girl."

Jaxon cocks his brow at me like I've lost my mind. "Yeah, but we're talking about Mindy, Lex. She's liable to tell the entire school Banner has genital warts if he pisses her off."

I let out a growl before turning and walking away from my aggravating friend. This is the problem. These guys get themselves involved with these shallow bitches and then can't handle the consequences. I love Banner, he's seriously one of the nicest guys—though you'd never know it based on his behavior—but when it comes to relationships and women, he's not from Mars, he's from Uranus.

"Where are you going, Lex?" Jax catches up to me. "And why are you so pissed? You know what that girl did to Drake. She's a bitch."

I stop and turn, feeling like we're right back where we started. In another fight because Jaxon fails to see my point again.

"Then he shouldn't have asked her out in the first place, Jax. But let me guess." I cross my arms. "He heard the rumor that she suctions like a vacuum, and he wanted to see if it was true. Am I right?"

The sheepish look on his face is all I need to know. Guys are so predictable. And they're all assholes. "You all are complete dicks. You know that? All you guys care about is sex. It's like none of you have the balls enough to handle a real relationship. Like you're all scared your dicks will shrivel up and die if you're forced to have sex with the same girl forever."

It's like they're all commitment phobes. Afraid they're going to be bored for the rest of their lives. Meanwhile, I just want to find the one person I can turn to no matter what. The one person I can cuddle up with when I have a bad day, and share exciting news with. And as far as sex goes, once you find an incredible partner, I don't think you ever grow tired of being with them. And if you do, then there are plenty of costumes and toys to bring the spice back.

He steps forward with his clenched jaw. His eyes now filled

with the same anger that's brewing inside my veins. "Don't you dare lump me in with them, Lex. I'm not scared of jack shit, and I sure as hell would never go out with a girl like Mindy just to get my dick sucked."

"Really?" I cock my chin. "Didn't you go out with Sienna just so you could pass your test? Isn't it kind of the same thing? You using a girl and then tossing her aside after you got what you wanted?"

"Are we really going there again?" he asks, shaking his head. "This is the last time I'm going to explain myself, Lex. I didn't seek Sienna out; she offered to help me. And there were no promises made for anything else, so my situation is not the same. Now, you need to reel the fucking attitude back in before I bend you over my knee and teach your ass a lesson on stubbornness."

A rush of heat spikes through my veins, making my cheeks suddenly feel flushed. I don't know why the idea of him following through with that threat is so hot, but my panties are now in danger of becoming soaked.

"You're calling me stubborn?" I ask. "Maybe you should be telling Banner to keep his dick locked in his pants. Maybe you shouldn't be encouraging his dickhead behavior."

"That's it," he growls, grabbing ahold of my arm. He turns and starts stomping toward his truck, dragging me in tow. He comes to a stop then opens the back door, lifting me up and shoving me inside. He climbs in after and I scoot back on the seat, unsure of his next move.

"You should know"—he inches forward, pinning me under his stare—"that I did tell Banner that. I told him he needed to lock his dick up and throw away the key." He shifts over me, hovering above, trapping me in. "You've gotten into this bad habit of assuming the worst of me, Lex. And it needs to stop. Now," he says, shifting back. "This stubborn ass of yours is going to pay for your bratty little outburst. And when I'm done with her, you better be on your knees apologizing for breaking your promise."

"What promise?" I gasp as he pulls me up and bends me over his lap. Man, he's strong. I didn't even see the maneuver coming.

"You said you'd never throw that Sienna shit in my face again, but you just did."

He's right. I did tell him I wouldn't bring it up again. But this situation with Banner triggered me.

"Damn," he groans as my skirt is shoved up to my back and the cool air hits my skin. "You really do have the most perfect ass, babe. It's so plump and round. A perky little treat that's going to be shiny red by the time I'm done with her."

His hands rub over my cheeks, deftly massaging, then suddenly there's a hard sting radiating my skin. "Ouch!" I shriek, trying to pull out from under him. "That hurt, Jaxon."

But in some weird way, it also felt good, sending a new type of pleasure running between my legs. It's like my body craves the discipline. Like the control he has is fueling my fire.

"It's a punishment, baby. It's supposed to teach you a lesson. If it felt good, you'd be defying me all the time. And what good would that do?"

Another smack lands down on the other cheek, and again, I let out a pained whimper. And again, there's that sizzling after effect that shudders through me. God, I'm sick. Not only do I crave Jaxon's harsh dominance, but I'm getting off on the pain too.

"Now, you're going to need to get this through your stubborn head, Lex." He spanks me again then runs his palm over the spot, smoothing out the sting. Making the burn spread to my clit and pulse in the spot. "I am not afraid of commitment. The idea of being with you for the rest of my life excites me. And it's all I want. So don't you dare accuse me of that shit again."

My body freezes up. My mind stuck on the word *you*. Did he just tell me he wants a relationship with me? Another spank lands down, and it snaps me out of my confused stupor. I struggle out of his hold, sitting up to face him. I need to see his eyes. I need to make sure my hope isn't misleading me. The dark lust that's overtaken his features plunders me, weakening every part of my body.

"What are you telling me, Jaxon Miller?" I need him to spell it out. Word for word.

He takes my cheeks in his hands, looking at me in a way he's never done before, and my heart skips a beat. "I'm saying that I'm in love with you, Lex. I'm saying that I want to spend the rest of my life with you. That I don't want to be your best friend, but I want to be your forever."

The world shifts on its axis. My heart racing. Mind orbiting as his words sink in. This is the moment I've been waiting for. What I'd hoped beyond hoped for.

Jaxon isn't just my best friend, he's my everything. He's the one I turn to when I'm having a bad day or need advice. He's the one I want to spend all my time with and miss if life gets busy. The one who makes me laugh when I'm down. Who makes me feel important and special. He's the love of my life. The boy I can't live without.

"You going to say something, Lex, or do I need to give you another spanking and teach you how to use your words?" He winks.

I finally get my mouth to cooperate and there's only one thing to say. "I love you."

As the words leave my lips, his head descends. Mouth smashing to mine. Kissing me like his life depends on it. He swallows me up, giving me his heart, taking mine in return. Twisting and stroking, tying us together with his tongue. Binding our love with the seal of his lips. And I finally understand what they mean by earth shattering. The world melts away and all that's left is us and the fire that's now blazing in my chest and burning its way throughout my body.

He grabs my waist, pulling me down onto his lap so I'm straddling his waist. Tugging me closer. Angling our heads so he can get deeper. Our tongues are ravenous. Mouths hungry. And the need is climbing fast. I've never been kissed like this before. I've never felt the pull in my belly, rising with every swipe across my tongue. It's like he's making love to my mouth. And I'm about to come. Closing in on the intense feeling.

"Need to get you home, babe," his rasp falls between my lips as he continues to numb my mind with his kiss. "Need my girl sprawled out so I can play with her sweet little cunt."

His hot words spike through me. My hips grinding down, seeking the friction, the pleasure. I can't stop. Home is too far. I can't wait that long. I need him to play with me now.

"No, Jax. Now," I breathe into him, lapping at him with equal fervor. My hands grip his hair as I work my pussy over his lap. The thin cotton between my legs is now soaked. No doubt making a mess of his lap too.

"Then take me for a ride."

I reach down between us, working frantically to get his jeans unfastened, but I need his help. "Jax," I groan, struggling to get the denim out of my way.

"I got you, babe."

He urges me to rise, then shoves his pants down around his thighs. As soon as his incredible cock springs free, I reach for him. This dick has been keeping my body restless for a week. God, he's so thick and warm. I stroke over him, relishing in the smoothness. Watering for a taste. So...I take one. I swipe my thumb over the little bead of cum sitting at the top and bring it up to my mouth. As I suck his flavor off my skin, he groans. His eyes burning hot and heavy.

"You need to get down on that dick, little one. His patience is about up."

I bite back my smirk, loving how crazy I make him. I lift my hips, pulling my panties to the side, too anxious to slide them down my legs. But Jaxon's hands come up under my skirt and tear them away from my body, ridding us of the problem. God, it's so sexy how he does that. The sheer power and strength are what I crave. His dominance feeds my sexual soul and makes me hungry for more.

His hands take hold of my thighs and guide me down to his cock, clearly losing patience for me to take the lead. But I love it when he's the one in control. As each of his thick inches breaches my entrance—fills me up—another wave of hot lust pools between my legs, coating his shaft.

"Damn," he groans, his head falling back on his shoulders, eyes squeezed shut. Teeth sinking into his lower lip. "This pussy is creaming me. She's a hot little mess."

I'd be ashamed if it weren't for the awe oozing from his voice. But I know he truly loves how wet I get for him.

"Now…" His eyes open, pupils dilated, heat burning darker. "You're going to grind this hot little pussy down on my dick and pay your respect. He didn't like you accusing him of being scared of commitment. Show him what he gets to look forward to for the rest of his life, babe. Give him a preview of his future."

His promise for a future ignites my need. I grip onto his shoulders and take the reins. Grinding in the love I have for him. Riding us to the goal line. Jaxon's hot words fueling me faster.

"That's it, my little Lexie Lou. Bounce on that dick like a good girl. Get me nice and dirty."

The pleasure climbs faster, the peak feeling higher this time. My hips gyrate like I'm twerking, taking us both up to the top. And when Jaxon rips my shirt down and sucks my nipple into his mouth, the pleasure snaps and I go crashing into my orgasm. Rocking through strums of heat, and taking Jaxon right along with me.

"Fuck, baby! God, that's it. Such a perfect little pussy."

He pumps up deeper, mouth latching back onto my breast and nursing me as we both ride through the shocks. When the final spark settles, I slump forward. My muscles completely limp. I've never had such an intense sexual connection with anyone. But I'm positive that's because I wasn't in love with any of the guys I slept with. Jaxon is my soul mate. He's the one my pussy was made for.

"I fucking love you, Lex."

I sit up, opening my eyes, trying to get my breathing under control. I brush my fingers over his cheeks, which are now flushed from his orgasm, making him look sexy as hell. "I love you too, Jax."

He reaches for my neck, pulling me to his lips, and when he kisses me, the fire ignites again. And now, I'm ready for him to take me home.

CHAPTER 13

Jaxon

"Jax!" my mom calls down to the basement. "The Graysons are here."

I nearly shoot off my bed, anxious to see my girl. Seven hours without her and I'm already going through withdrawals. But we're going to have to play it cool tonight. We don't want our parents finding out we're a couple just yet. Knowing them, they'll start enforcing the open-door policy whenever we're together and keep us from having our sleepovers. And I honestly don't want Mr. Grayson giving me the evil eye every time we're together, worried that I'm violating his little girl. Lex is his pride and joy, and you know how dads can be about their little girls.

I walk into the living room and get blasted by a wave of hot need the moment I see my little one dressed in my football jersey and a pair of cheer shorts. It's like my two favorite things wrapped in one: my girl and football.

"Hey, Jax!" she says, hitting me with that smile that fuels my heart. I can feel it already pounding like a drum. The blood rushing south. My cheeks heating as the beast comes to the surface, recalling all the things we did last night. She's like my personal genie, making my every desire come true. Proving to be my unrealized fantasy. God, she's incredible.

"Jaxon." My mom's voice has me snapping out of my sexual train of thought. I turn and look at her and see the curious look on my mom's face. "Aren't you going to say hello? Please tell me you two aren't fighting again."

I shake my head. "How'd you know we were in a fight?"

Both moms laugh, and our dads have smirks on their faces. "Because you weren't attached at the hip last week. It was obvious something was going on."

"Now, did you two make up or do we need to have an intervention?" my mom asks.

"No," I tell her, although a sexual intervention may be needed at the moment. My dick is about to make an embarrassment out of me. "We worked it out."

"Good," Mrs. Grayson says. "We were worried for a moment. It's been years since you two have fought. Now..." She turns toward my mom. "Can I help you get the table set?"

The two women dart off to the kitchen and Lex comes over, wrapping her arms around me like she usually does. Only problem is, her simple touch is causing me to make a mess of myself.

"Come on, Lex. Why don't we go down and finish that movie we started last week while they get dinner ready?"

She nods and I lead her down into my cave, closing the door behind us just in case. The second I have her alone, I slam her up against the wall and dive in for her sweet mouth. Her little moan strikes a chord and I lift her up, wrapping her around my waist, then carry her over to my bed and drop her in the center of it.

"You're a naughty girl, Lexie Lou."

"Why's that?" she asks, her siren voice breathless and wanton.

"You showed up in my jersey and now I'm hard as a rock."

I climb onto the bed, scooting forward, gripping onto her shorts and pulling them down her legs. Another sweet moan falls from her lips and has me worried that my wild girl is going to be giving us up to the parents if I don't do something to cover her sexy sounds.

"Alexa, turn on my music."

"Turning on music," the electronic box answers, then my workout playlist begins to play.

I move in, pushing Lexie's thighs apart and see her bare little cunt already coated in that sweet nectar that I'm now addicted to. She didn't even bother wearing panties today. Probably on account of me shredding them all to pieces. I can't help myself. The beast takes over and the need wins out every time.

I crawl forward and burrow between her thighs, lapping at her wet little pussy. Savoring her flavor. Lexie's moan is as hungry as my mouth. She loves the way I eat her out. Told me she'd never been able to get off that way before. Which surprised me.

I'm not sure what the other fuckers she dated were doing down here, because she goes off like a rocket within seconds for me. I'm just thankful I can give her what she needs. Because she sure as hell gives me what I need. Sex has never been so fire before. My dick is now going to forever weep at her feet, begging for her incredible attention. Mouth, tits, pussy, ass. Every part of her is an endless treasure trove of pleasure. And I can't get enough.

Her hips thrust up, pussy grinding against my mouth and chin. It seems like she's ready for more, so I pull her folds apart with my thumbs and thrust my tongue inside her hole. The sexual cry she lets out has me driving forward. Tongue fucking her tight little cunt with abandon. Her juices running down my chin. She's close. I can feel it, which means it's time for my final trick.

I slip my pinky back to her rear entrance and dip it inside. As soon as I'm wedged into her little puckered star, she goes off like a rocket. My name falling from her lips. Back bowing off my bed. Pussy quivering against my mouth. Damn, she drives me insane. Just watching her come makes my nuts draw up like they're ready to bust.

"Jaxon," she breathes as I give her one last kiss and slide up her body. "That mouth."

I smile, knowing that she's addicted too. In the future, if we ever find ourselves in a fight again, I know exactly what will win her back in my favor. I'll just flip her over, give her a hot little spanking for being difficult, then plunge my tongue inside her heat and fuck the anger right out of her.

"Hey, kids." My mom's voice has me shooting up. "It's time for dinner."

"You go on up," I whisper to Lex, sliding her shorts back up into place. "I need to run to the bathroom and will be up in a minute."

Her smile turns into a frown and she shoots up in the bed. "You're going to take care of him without me?" She reaches into my joggers and locks around my cock. "That's not fair, Jax."

I know she's jealous of the fact, but I don't have a choice. There's no way I'm walking into that room with a tent in my pants.

"Do you want your dad finding out exactly what I want to do with his daughter?" I groan as she gives me a squeeze. Honestly, one more minute of her greedy hand stroking me and I'll be done.

"I want this dick of yours inside me."

Shit! Now I'm done for. I flip her onto her back, slide those shorts right back down her legs then slide inside her tight heat. I fuck her hard and fast. Charging straight to the end zone.

Nothing and no one standing in my way of scoring. And in a matter of seconds, I'm filling her tight pussy up with my seed, making a mess out of the both of us. And she's coming right along with me. Her trigger super sensitive and quick, which is perfect for moments like these.

"Jaxon?" my dad calls this time, causing me to shoot off the bed. "Dinner's getting cold. You two need to quit with the make-up sex and get the hell up here, boy."

Holy shit! Lexie's eyes bulge from their sockets, cheeks turning dark red from embarrassment. My stomach twists up with nervous tension. It's obvious our parents heard us, which makes this entire situation super awkward. And puts me in a bad place with her dad.

"Coming," I say.

"You already did that," he calls back. "Now get the hell up here."

We quickly get our act together, doing our best to look as normal as we can, slowly ascending the stairs, dread hitting the closer we get to the top. I feel like I'm heading to my doom and nervous like hell to see the look on Mr. Grayson's face. We walk into the kitchen and our moms burst into a fit of giggles, no wine in sight. I glance over at Lex, totally confused. I'd thought they'd be pissed.

"Rule number one," my mom states as we take our seats, biting back her laugh and trying to appear serious. "No kids until you're done with school. It's too hard to chase your dreams and raise a family at the same time."

I'm shocked by her remark, but I one hundred percent agree with her words of advice.

"Rule number two," Mrs. Grayson chimes in, trying to bite back her laugh too. "We both get to help you pick out your wedding dress when you two get married."

"Mom!" Lex gasps. "No one said anything about getting married."

I turn to my girl, narrowing my stare on her stunning brown eyes. "We're definitely getting married, Lex, so you better get on board with your mom's rule."

My girl turns to me, the biggest smile lighting up her face before she narrows me with a stern look of her own. "That better not be your proposal, Jax."

I shake my head, chuckling. "No, babe. I'm just giving you a heads-up so there's no mistaking my intentions. Need us both on the same page."

The aws from our moms send a wave of embarrassment straight to my cheeks. I need to remember our parents are in the room and are eagerly listening. I still haven't been able to make eye contact with her father. I'm afraid he wants to murder me right about now.

"Told you my boy was a genius," my dad says, shooting Mr. Grayson his big cheesy grin.

"Yep," Mr. Grayson says, shocking me with his response. I finally turn in his direction and see the matching grin on his face. "You were right. But I still think my daughter is smarter. She chose your son, after all."

The tension unravels in my stomach. My shoulders finally settling. It looks like I'm officially one of the family now.

While our parents start in on their teasing banter, fighting over whose got the superior genes, I look over at my girl who's radiating with love and happiness.

"I love you," I mouth.

"Love you two," she mouths back, and my heart beats like a snare drum.

CHAPTER 14

Lexie

"This party is epic, Jax!" Samantha shouts over the loud music, all of our friends chiming in in agreement.

It really is. Jaxon went all out this year. Every part of his house is filled with creepy dolls. It's almost as haunted looking as the Fright House. And to top it off, he went and hired my favorite local band: The Poor Kids.

"Come on, Sammy Cakes," Drake says. "It's time for you to dance with me."

I shake my head, as he drags her onto the makeshift dance floor. I'm still completely shocked how those two ended up together. But something happened between them on Fright Night, and ever since, they've been locked at the hip—and the lips.

"What the heck is she doing here?"

Mercy's shocked gasp has me turning. Walking through the front door is Sienna.

"Shit," I hear Jax whisper. "I forgot she was coming tonight."

I turn, looking up at him, not understanding how he knew she'd be here. I sure as hell didn't send the girl an invitation.

He shakes his head, reaching for me, his Adam's apple bobbing. "Before you freak the fuck out, Lex, please let me explain, babe."

I hold my tongue, knowing that I need to hear him out. I didn't do that the last time and we almost lost our friendship over it.

"In exchange for helping me on my test, Sienna asked if she could come to the party since all of her friends were invited. I told her okay at the time, not thinking it through. But I'm going to go tell her to leave. I'm sorry, baby. I would've uninvited her, but I completely forgot she was coming. I've been a little distracted lately."

He goes to turn, but I stop him, shaking my head. "You don't have to apologize, Jax. And you don't have to tell her to leave. I don't care that she's here."

His brow shoots up to his hairline, looking shocked by my response. The thing is... He was right. Sienna's a bitch and anything she does or says is insignificant. I was the one giving her power. Letting her have an affect on my life. But now, I'm never going to do that again. The only one that holds any power over me is the incredible man before me.

He steps up closer, his huge frame looming over me. Looking every bit the Viking War Lord he's dressed as. "You need to come with me, little one." His intense whisper has my knees weakening. I'm always starved for his dominance. "I have a special present for you."

I take his hand, locking my fingers with his, and let him guide me through the crowd and downstairs to his bedroom. As soon as we're locked inside his room, he spins me around and pins me against the door, kissing the hell out of me and leaving me panting.

"One day, I'm going to give you the biggest diamond I can

find," he whispers against my lips. "But for now, I want you to wear this."

His hands come up to my neck and he's holding a black leather collar with a heart-shaped silver pendant dangling from it. A flutter of excitement rushes in when I see his last name engraved in the center, etched in bold. It's a stamp of ownership, even more significant than any diamond ring.

"You're mine." His voice is fierce. "And now everyone will know it."

My body ignites. I turn to face the wall, pulling my hair out of his way so he can put it around my neck. He locks it in place then I feel him sliding down my back, dropping to his knees. My skirt slides up my legs and a shudder of need rocks through me. His low growl at the sight of my bare skin weakening me further.

"So fucking perfect."

Suddenly, his head is burrowing between my cheeks and a needful moan tears from my throat as he begins to shamelessly lap at my rear entrance. Making me dizzy with need. Devouring me as if his life depends on it. The things he does to me are what secret fantasies are made of. Forbidden desires that no one ever wants to admit. And it drives me crazy.

Jax torments me with his tongue. His groans growing heavier. His hands gripping me tighter.

"Bend more for me, baby." His demanding grunt has me falling forward, obeying his command. And then... my cheeks are spread wide in his firm grip and his tongue starts drilling into my forbidden hole.

The need powering through him pushes me forward and drives me right over the edge. I shatter. His name shouting from my lips. Nails clawing at the door as the pleasure crawls up each and every nerve. Flames tearing through my body. It's so good. Too good. And I can't get enough. I never want it to stop.

"It's time, little one." His hot words hit my ear as I fight to come back down. "This tight little hole"—his fingers rub over the tingling spot, one pushing its way in—"is going to split for me." His finger starts pumping in an out, working me back up into that tormented state of hunger.

"She's going to be a good girl and pucker up around my cock." Another finger sinks inside. "Let her master drill into her hard and deep."

The need almost swallows me whole. My body is about to give out. The door is supporting all of my weight as he pumps in faster. His dirty mouth commanding my pleasure.

"She's going to behave as I fill her up. And when I'm done marking her," his teeth sink into my neck on a growl, fingers pushing and pulling me up to the brink, stretching me wider, "You're going to climb onto my face and let me tickle that clit with my tongue."

"Jax!" My moan falls against the cold wooden door as my tongue starts searching for friction. He grips my chin, jerking my head to the side then swallows my mouth whole. Sucking on me until I'm gasping for air. He releases me on a growl and steps back.

"Get down on all fours and crawl to the bed, little one."

God, I love his domination. I slip down to the floor and follow my orders. Crawling slowly. My butt on full display for him as he shadows my movement. I glance back over my shoulder, wanting to see his approval. His hand is stroking his long cock in a tight grip. His eyes locked on my ass, lust burning so hot in his stare that my juices begin flowing down my thigh.

I get to the bed and climb up onto the mattress, moving to the center and waiting for my next command.

"Such a good girl," he praises, coming to the side of the bed, and admiring the view. His hand reaches forward and my top is yanked down, my tits now hanging free. His fingers tighten around my nipple and begin to tweak the pleasure right from my body. My head falls forward from the weight of need trying to pull me back under.

"These little babies are so sensitive." He gives me a tight pinch. "I can't wait for the clamps to arrive." *Oh God, me too.* "I'll get to pull on that chain as I take you for a ride." He reaches for the other, making sure she isn't left out. "Damn. It's time, baby."

He drops his hand and then turns to his nightstand, grabbing the lube out of his drawer. I watch him squirt some into his hand and lather his heavy equipment until it's slick and shiny. His eyes roam over every inch of my body as he strokes. The pleasure clenching his jawline.

Finally, he climbs onto the bed, positioning himself behind me, and those lubed fingers are back at my rear entrance. Penetrating me with heat, getting me nice and ready to take him in. I'm more than ready. The ache is at a painful state. And if he doesn't fuck me now, I'm going to lose my mind.

Just as I'm about to beg for it, I feel the pressure, pushing in slowly, opening me up little by little. His low groan rumbles through me. His grip on me tightening as he fights to restrain himself. He's trying to go slow but his need is fierce.

I decide to take control and push back, giving him permission to take what he needs. The pressure shoots up my spine as he sinks in deeper. "Careful, baby," he grunts. "I don't want to hurt you."

There's only a tiny bit of pain, but my body is adjusting. Fast. And when his hand wraps around to my front and his fingers begin playing with my clit, I completely open up for him, allowing him to fully sink inside. I'm not going to last long. The heat is already taking hold. The pleasure pumping through me as he begins to thrust.

"That's it, little one. You're being such a good girl." He picks up the pace, rubbing my clit in circles as he fucks into me. "My bare-bottom little beauty giving her master such a good squeeze."

The sizzle starts to flood in, embers of heat flickering at the edges. I'm close.

"Now, hold tight, because I'm about to show you who owns this ass."

His fingers release my clit, both of his hands gripping onto my hips, and then... he's fucking me hard and fast, shattering me into pieces and sending me straight into the inferno. I can barely hold myself up, am barely clinging to consciousness. The feeling is so intense. The pleasure extreme. And it doesn't cease. It keeps coming and coming.

"God, Lex," his groan breaks through my roaring senses. "You're so fucking amazing." He is too. Amazing isn't even a strong enough word to describe the way he makes me feel. "You're mine, baby." He pulls me into his embrace, kissing my shoulder.

"Forever and always," I whisper, grabbing onto his hair, still struggling to catch my breath. I'll never be anyone else's. Not in this lifetime or the next.

* * *

"THERE YOU TWO ARE," Piper says, giving me a knowing look. She's one to talk. I saw her and that stepbrother of hers parked out front for an awfully long time before they decided to come inside and join the party.

"Have you seen Ava?" I ask, wondering if she's finally arrived. She texted that she was running late, but that was hours ago.

"She's here." Piper nods. "Just saw her heading out back if you're looking for her."

"I'm gonna run out and say hi to her real quick."

As soon as I step into the backyard, I'm greeted by screams. Looks like the varsity guys are giving the guests quite a fright out here. People are running around the graveyard, dodging the reapers, but I don't see Ava anywhere. I start to turn to head back inside, but stop. There she is. Walking out toward the "haunted" woods. Alone.

I start heading towards her but am suddenly caught around the waist.

"Going somewhere, little one?"

Jaxon's deep voice has my nerves calming. I thought for a second one of the guys was getting handsy. But it's only *my* guy getting handsy.

"I was just trying to catch up with Ava. She's heading out into the woods."

"Do you think you could hold that thought for a sec and come with me? The Poor Kids are getting ready to play my special request."

I smile, taking his hand and let him lead me back in the house. Right as we enter the living room, the lead singer starts talking into the microphone.

"And this next one goes out to Lexie. From your best friend and your forever."

The tears spring to my eyes as Jaxon's arms wrap around my back and pull me into his chest, swaying us back and forth while we're serenaded with my favorite song of all time. This is what love is all about. This is what matters most. Us.

And one day...when I'm dressed in my white dress and Jaxon's wearing his sexy-as-hell tux, this is going to be the first song we'll dance to as husband and wife.

EPILOGUE

❧

10 years later
Lexie

"Okay, class. Remember to stay with your trusted adult tonight and have your parents check your candy before you eat any," I say in my serious voice, otherwise, it will go in one ear and out the other.

All my little monsters nod eagerly, ready to be dismissed from class so they can go and get to trick-or-treating. I grab my bag of goodies and hold the door open, making sure as each little munchkin passes, they know how great they did today. Their special little "Thriller" performance for the retirement community was such a hit. And all the senior citizens who were able to join us today had the biggest smiles on their faces, melting my heart and making me so proud of each and every one of them.

"Bye, Mrs. Miller," Laney says, giving me her big toothy grin. I kneel down so we're eye level and give her a kiss on the cheek.

"You did so great today, Laney. Your pirouettes were right on point."

She smiles even bigger, looking up at her mom. "Did you hear that, Mommy? I did really good today."

Sienna smiles down at her sweet daughter. "Yes, you did, angel. You were absolutely beautiful, and the entire class did an amazing job."

My heart overflows with joy as I see the sparkle in Laney's eyes from her mother's compliment. Somewhere along the way, the past finally caught up with Sienna, and she realized what was truly important in life. The day she showed up on my doorstep, apologizing for all the things she did and said back when we were kids, I thought an apocalypse had come and she'd been body snatched. But in truth, what finally made her realize her error was getting out from under her mother's thumb. And I think that husband of hers had something to do with it.

"Thanks, Lex. You all put on such a fun performance," she says, taking her daughter's hand. "I can't wait to see your Christmas Spectacular."

"It's going to be amazing." I smile broadly. "And your little Laney is going to have a very special part." I wink at the sweetest little girl. Laney doesn't know it yet, but I'm going to make her the lead in the performance.

"Okay, well, we better run so we can get to the fun," Sienna says.

They both head out, and I lock up behind them. Since it's Halloween, I decided not to hold the evening classes tonight. The teenagers want to be out with their friends, anyway.

"You know, you should always make sure the studio is empty before you lock yourself alone inside with a monster." The deep voice startles me, nearly giving me a heart attack. I turn and see my husband hiding in the shadows, lurking in the dark like a predator. And judging by the Grim Reaper costume he's wearing, I think that's exactly why he showed up tonight: to attack.

"Where's Joel?" I ask, unable to stay in character until I know where our son is.

"He's safe," he states, stepping out of the darkness. His huge frame a fierce weapon against my sexual defenses. "His grandparents are no doubt filling him up with sugar so that he'll be a little hellion when we go to pick him up later."

I roll my eyes at that. Our parents love spoiling their grandson rotten because they know that at the end of the day, they get to hand him back over and we're the ones that get to deal with the little terror.

"Did you know that Halloween is when the monsters come out to play?"

I take a step back, knowing he's getting ready to strike. My body's already hot, and my leotard is slowly turning into a wet mess between my legs. It's harder these days to find time to play. Between Jaxon's company, my studio, and of course our son, time is limited. But when we do find the time, it's mind-blowing. And always worth the wait.

"You keep backing away from me, little one. Haven't you learned by now that if you come willingly, your punishment won't be so harsh?"

He stalks forward, eliminating the space between us. I take another step back, and find myself up against the mirrors. Jaxon takes the final stride and is looming over me, his huge frame trapping me against the glass.

"You've been chosen, little one. And there's no place for you to hide. But if you get down on your knees and beg, then I may let you come."

I slide my back down the glass, taking myself to my knees. His dark cloak parts at the side and then his huge staff is revealed. Bare and completely hard and ready. His hand comes up to the top of my head and then he pulls me forward, guiding me right to where my mouth is needed.

My body shudders in pleasure as his giant staff parts my lips and slides to the back of my throat, his grip in my hair tightening, and a loud bellowing groan echoes throughout the space.

I pull myself off his cock and then go back down, relishing in the sweet torment that I'm causing him, licking up every drop of his seed as it dribbles out. It's obvious by how heavy his balls are, that he's been weighted down with this load for a while, and when he comes, it's going to be hard and fierce.

"That's good, little angel. Just like that." I take him all the way to the back of my throat again, bobbing on his stiff cock. My body growing to a feverish ache. Then suddenly, his grip tightens in the back of my hair and he's pulling me off and up from the ground. "You did good, but that's not going to save your soul. Now, you have five seconds to run, but if I catch you, you're mine."

He releases his hold and I take off in a near sprint, heading out the back door and down the side alleyway. I'm about to reach the main street when Jaxon appears before me, blocking my path. He must've gone out the front, knowing exactly which way I'd run.

"Tsk...tsk, little one. Looks like you were too slow."

I turn to run back inside my studio but am caught before I reach the door. Jaxon pressing me up against the wall and ripping away the material between my legs. The cool night air blows over my overheated skin and a chill runs down my spine. With a wild grunt, I'm suddenly invaded. Jaxon's huge dick rams into me, sending a jolt of pleasure into the deepest crevice of my soul. I love it when he's rough and wild. When the beast comes out to play. It still drives me just as crazy as it did when we were young.

"I'll make you a deal, Lexie Miller." His deep voice is right at my ear, his heaving chest pressed against my back while my breasts are getting pinched and grabbed by his vicious hands. "If you let me fill you up with my seed and bear me another child, then I'll let you keep your soul."

Oh my God! Is he saying what I think he's saying? I turn my head, looking up into my incredible husband's eyes. And there, in the depths of his loving stare, I see it. He's telling me he wants another baby. He's asking if it's okay.

We had both decided after Joel was born that we were done having kids. Both of us had been only children growing up so we wanted to give our son the same special attention that we had had. Plus, it was hard with both of us trying to get our businesses off the ground. But now that everything's running smoothly, and our little guy is in preschool, it feels like there's room in our life for more.

I'd been wanting to bring up the subject of another kid for a few months, but didn't want to add more stress on Jaxon's plate. But right now, he's asking me to make him a dad again. And I'm more than ready.

"I love you," I whisper, feeling his cock expand as the words leave my mouth. "I love you so much, Jaxon Miller. And I'm ready for another."

His smile makes my heart soar. "Not as much as I love you, Lexie Lou."

He leans forward, pressing a kiss to my lips, stealing my breath away with the love that he pours into me. I never imagined when I was a little girl, being chased by the boy who would always steal my candy and pull my hair, that I'd end up here. Living this incredible life. Having a love so full of heat and compassion that it makes my toes curl just thinking about it. And I definitely never would've dreamt that that same boy, my best friend, would be chasing me down a dark alleyway and fucking me senseless against the wall. But here we are.

He thrusts up into me fast and hard, his fingers pressed to my clit, rubbing me with just the right amount of pressure, and I find a new level of ecstasy, a new high that sends my heart on a galloping chase and takes me right over the edge. And as the fireworks explode inside my veins, the pleasure tearing through me like a storm, I fall deeper in love with my childhood best friend. The man who's made all my dreams come true.

ACKNOWLEDGMENTS

Thank You!

I'd like to thank all those special people in my life who have not only cheered me on, but who have had tremendous patience with my process. To my hubby, kiddos, friends and family... I love you all.

And, of course, to my editor Erica Russikoff. Thank you so much for always polishing up my work and fixing my semi-colons. LOL. I'm blessed to have you on my team.

Lastly, I'd like to thank all of my readers. You all are the reason I do this. So, thank you for reading!

Hugs,
Landry

ABOUT THE AUTHOR

Landry Hill Spends most of her days fantasizing and bringing book boyfriends to life in ink. When she's not writing about sexy alphas who love hard and spoil their women in every single delicious way, she's busy being a cheerleader for her kiddos and a devoted wife to her own sexy-bearded alpha.

She's a true believer in Love and Romance. Cherishes her friendships. And knows that happy endings don't just exist between the pages of a book. They also exist in real life.

And... Between the sheets. (wink, wink)

Landry's Website

ALSO BY LANDRY HILL

THE CAPRIZIO FAMILY

I Don't

I Know

I Won't

I Promise

I Will

DIRTY COPS

Resisting

THE FRIGHT SERIES

Fright House

Fright Night

Fright Bash

Fright Fest

Fright Ball

Fright Girl

Printed in Dunstable, United Kingdom